i

Catch a Wagon
to the Stars

Thomas F. Sheehan

Pocol Press

Fairfax, VA

POCOL PRESS
Published in the United States of America
by Pocol Press
3911 Prosperity Avenue
Fairfax, VA 22031
www.pocolpress.com

Publisher's Cataloguing-in-Publication

Names: Sheehan, Thomas F., 1928, author.
Title: Catch a wagon to the stars / Thomas F. Sheehan.
Description: Fairfax, VA: Pocol Press, 2018.
Identifiers: ISBN 978-1-929763-84-9 | LCCN 2018954126
Subjects: LCSH Frontier and pioneer life--West (U.S.)--Fiction. |
Cowboys--Fiction. | West (U.S.)--Fiction. | Short stories, American. |
Western stories. | Historical fiction. | BISAC FICTION / Westerns |
FICTION / Short Stories (single author).
Classification: LCC PS3569.H39216 C38 2018 | DDC 813.6--dc23

Library of Congress Control Number: 2018954126

ACKNOWLEDGEMENTS

Tom Sheehan's stories have appeared in *Rope and Wire Western Lifestyle Magazine, Western Online,* and *Literally Stories.*

TABLE OF CONTENTS

When Corporal Newton "Newt" Tewksbury, aboard ship while crossing the Atlantic Ocean but Boston-born, and later an army bugler, hurt his hand in 1848 in the War with Mexico, he was discharged from service. He figured he didn't have to go far to a section of the west where he always had a hankering to be on his own. *Further north* drew him across the rolling plains of the Texas Panhandle toward Iowa, which had become a state only two years earlier, *and he took his bugle with him.*

His thin sparse hair made him look better in a hat, and the sombrero and prominent high cheekbones brought a keen green and an alert light to his eyes. Even with that gift, his lips were best expressed when pursed on the mouthpiece of the horn, which might well have been born as part of his body, or his personality, take a pick.

On the way northeast north, he played different bugle calls at odd hours, free of the Army's directives concerning time or occasion. Now and then he'd earn a salute from a passerby or from those he joined en route, surely ex-military in either case, when he let loose with "Reveille" or "To the Colors" or "Taps", as though the listeners had earned the honors or knew the intentions of the bugle calls.

He knew a soft glee at first, and then an explosive sense of gratitude and pure excitement at being able to deliver his talent to the wide-open outdoors.

Playing the bugle for hundreds or thousands of soldiers had been an articulation.

Now, journey-wise, to him, it was the same for a lone listener, a distant rider at a search, a lone miner seeking a change in lifestyle, a vagabond tossed adrift.

In a range of hills on the horizon in lower Iowa, he spotted three riders, each on a separate hill, who waved in recognition of his sudden "Call to Colors", the prior urge to let it loose from his bugle. He was thrilled at the reception from three points at one time, even if accidental in nature, but ecstatic at the messages coming back from obvious veterans in-the-know out in the world, and dearly wished they could all ride up to one campsite, sit around the fire, tell their stories. A kind of deliciousness touched at his ears, at his soul.

Again, in a narrow box canyon the next day, the urge for sending out "Taps" emanated from his loneliness, the images of lost comrades still haunting him, and bare moments later a fusillade of shots replied from an unseen site in the canyon. The former corporal waved his bugle in hopes some lone soul, responsible for the shots, might appear. And marveled that another sincere connection had been accomplished in the mostly barren wilds spread out before him.

1

No lone soul appeared, but Tewksbury was highly pleased at the reception and pleased no end that he was toting the bugle. Hope came that it would introduce him to some fine folks in Iowa.

He was willing to bet on it.

But gamblers, we know, unless they are cheaters, lose more often than they win, and we can bet on that.

Another feeling began beating in him, that he'd be blessed or cured by certain bugle calls, for each one was recognizable from its first note depending on those who listened and their location at reception. All previous calls in his ken had been in earshot of regular military settings, a post or station, a skirmish line, in the dark of night or in the light of dawn, in the mysterious ways of wind at its universal work, at the rush of sound it carried, at the hope enriched in the rocky glens or the open grass, the places where music might have another name but not another mission … and he somehow believed he had a duty, a cause, in his destiny, but didn't know what it was or where it went.

The old thought repeated itself, and he had tried so often, but he had no voice to spread a song to any listeners, to or for their hungry ears, where a soul might sit right up and demand a sense of music if not a song in itself, but he had his bugle; it would do his singing for him no matter who or where that audience made an appearance.

These quandaries were part of his haunting, his loneliness, the sense of loss that may ride horseback on a lone soul about in the universe where a canyon or a cave or a cliff face meant as much as the morning sun, a month-old moon, or a new star blinking in the corner of an eye.

Each day, by chance or accident, an opportunity arose which required his intervention with his bugle, and always from some high point in the landscape the way chance comes on us with its deep purpose to test the souls of all man.

From one rise above a stream he spotted a couple, man and woman, washing themselves while enjoying a swim in the river. Newt assumed them to be husband and wife or long lovers, as they hastened into each other's arms as soon as they were out of the water. This act was also spotted by three more riders who dismounted and started creeping from tree to tree to get near the couple locked in deep embrace. Their intentions appeared obvious to Newt, who had a higher regard for women than they did.

He swung the bugle to his lips and delivered "Tattoo" as robustly as he could, alarming the couple, both of whom grabbed their weapons and clothes and sought shelter from public view. The three cowards, in the face of weapons, remounted and disappeared from view.

Newt blew a few loose notes to bid adieu as he parted from the sight of those who had been alarmed by his bugle call.

A few days later, from another high rise where he was always alert to the land that lay below him, he spotted a stagecoach coming along its route far below and also saw beyond the next bend a group of riders gathered behind a huge rocky formation, in nothing less than a threatening hold-up waiting to happen. Their threat was odious.

No panic grabbed the former corporal, but the phalanx of calls whistled through his mind for the most proper and obvious one to use as a warning. He pulled the bugle off his saddle mount and broke loose with "Retreat", the notes ringing downhill its melody *to cease action, come to a stand-still, pay attention* hoping an old veteran was at the reins or aboard the stagecoach and understood the directive; he also fired a single shot in the air.

Stock-still in the saddle he sat, as the stagecoach came to a grudging stop a couple of minutes later, and Newt fired a second round from his pistol to a point somewhere ahead of the stagecoach. The round bounced off a rock face, as an added warning to pay attention. When the coach stopped, two passengers climbed to the top rack and waved handguns in the air. Ahead of them, around the bend, four hidden horsemen rode off in the other direction, the surprise robbery attempt aborted from afar.

"Well, stranger," said one of the top rack passengers, at meeting Newt Tewksbury, "I heard about you down the road, or someone like you, riding around the country with a bugle in his hand. That you or another vet of the war? I'm damned glad to meet you, Newt. What outfit was you?"

With a slight puff in his chest, Newt said, "Bugler, 1st Regiment, Pennsylvania Volunteers, Colonel Francis Wynkoop our top man. I was separated last year, I think, time jumping quick steps for me."

A quick laugh was followed by, "My name's Hugo Brant, Pennsylvania 11th. Glad to meet you and I'm not dumping any crap in your lap about buglers. It's either another one of you or your story's beating the bushes. Hell, you might be getting famous around here. I hope everybody pays you mind. We're heading on now to Cotters Grove in Iowa, up-trail ahead of us, near a days' ride."

He shook hands again, the shaking as thorough as the first one, a wide smile on his face, his teeth a brilliant white against his darker skin, his gray-green eyes lit up with appreciation.

As Newt studied Brent, he wondered what he looked like to this other veteran because he hadn't looked into a mirror since he took off his uniform. He'd have to take care of that if he met any more people like Brent, direct, responsive, *been around the Horn,* so to speak. He had not thought of appearance, he had not thought about meeting people … not for a long while, but both must come to account.

3

Newt offered his observation even as he awaited the reaction: "There were four of them up ahead. All four took off the other way, northwest, like a trail off the main route, two black horses, two paints, all at a gallop."

"After all of this, I'm sure there's some great things in store for you," Brent said. "You're a different dude, that's for sure, different as all get out." Looking around, he shook Newt's hand again, and said, "We're going now, pard, but it's been a pleasure meeting you."

Newt kept a thought to himself, that Hugo Brent would have been a great comrade in the war; the old images sat still in his mind. One of his problems, he knew, was he remembered a lot of them from the past, and it was too late to do any good for many of them, if any, if ever. Losing a comrade like Hugo Brent was the saddest part of war, not that death wasn't far away from you at any time, around any corner, being muzzle-loaded this very instance from a point you could throw a rock at and hit.

A sudden new thought told him that this indeed might also be a farewell, like the last time he'd ever see this new comrade of sorts on the open trail to wherever.

Changes come along, sometimes as quick as breath changes, and he was soon riding into the little town of Cotters Grove and dropping the reins over a saloon rail and with another change of breath was ordering a beer from a smiling barkeep who slyly noted the trail duds and general conditions of a new customer with a thirst to be satisfied.

Newt was at his second sip when an unpleasant and unfinished attempt at a bugle note came from outside. He bolted from the saloon to find a youngster pressing his army bugle to his lips, clumsy as a bull moose.

"That's something you shouldn't do, son, take something off somebody's saddle like it's your own. That's a whole lot of not right, if you can understand me 'cause that bugle belongs to me. It's my property now and into The Forever, and put your mind to that, son. It'll do you good."

He felt like a teacher and he didn't want to be a teacher, but wanted to be a student, all the time learning like this little shaver was, learning the ropes, the brands, the tricks of a trade all the way to the very end of Time.

"I just wanted to try it, mister," the boy said. "I heard all about you from the stagecoach guys talking about you. They was real excited, kept telling how you saved them from a hold-up just blowin' on the horn. I can't wait 'til I tell my Pa when he gets back. He's on a drive." His stubby finger pointed back over his shoulder to the north.

The boy handed the bugle to Newt and said, "Please, mister, play it for me. I never heard one."

His sombrero in miniature sat on the back of his head, his face was full of expectant glee as he looked around at the group of people gathering in front of the saloon, some folks coming out of the saloon, some from across the street, even the barber had hung up his strop and him and his customer joined the massing group.

The boy, indeed, had a strange effect on Newt, warm as the sun, honest as the honest injun to be found, glee and joy and expectation gleaming on his face, and all of manhood facing him before he knew it, with a horse, a girl, a job to become good at, friends to be found, trusted, loved; the same places and things Newt Tewksbury had found or had been in his short time here in the New World of the Old World.

Someone in the midst of the crowd said "Amen" and broke up Newt's small reverie, somebody else started to clap, and life in one big swallow seemed to jump clear down Newt Tewksbury's throat. The saloon owner said, "Play as long as you want, mister, as short as you want, but your drinks are all on me, all day. Ever last one of 'em." He looked around him as the whole lot of customers in the saloon had formed behind him outside the swinging door.

A bunch of "Amens" followed from the crowd, now getting bigger by the very minute, so former Corporal Newt Tewksbury gave the crowd at Cotters Grove, Iowa the full run of his bugle calls repertoire, identifying each one before he played it, and him enjoying a few eyes that began to water right there in front of him, in front of the saloon, in front of the whole town it seemed, without a single bit of embarrassment.

He knew he had a job to do, had a place here in this world whether it was right here in this place or in another place, a job, a duty, a responsibility that weighed its ton or so on top of his little piece of Life in the West, a long way from the wide Atlantic and Boston itself.

After several renditions and explanations, most of the crowd could recognize, from the first notes, "First Call", "Reveille", "Assembly", "Mail Call", "Mess Call", "Retreat", "To the Colors", "Tattoo", "Call to Quarters" and "Taps", leaving out a bunch of others only real students would ask for down the line.

The boy, Darren Goodwin, was ecstatic and begged to be taught how to play the horn, "just like you, Mister Newt. Just like you."

Darren, in time, just like Newt Tewksbury, became an exceptional bugler, and earned his own fame all the way to Chicago. Cotters Grove became a central point of bugle dispersion across the west, Newt Tewksbury at the head of it all, until death took him in its arms when he was about to celebrate his 92nd birthday, the army bugle in one hand, his lungs fighting for a final breath, and his last words, "I made do."

Sheriff Greg Gardenhire felt the saddle loosen under him as he forded a rocky section of Montana's Madison River just below Canyon Ferry Lake where three rivers start their name calling. He didn't think the saddle would leave him as abruptly as it did, with him in the water and the saddle heading with a sudden rush toward a tightly-packed spot on the river, canyon walls rising so close together they might once have been a singular structure. He had no fear he'd be able to retrieve his saddle at that point no matter how strong the river flow was, a place where rugged wall clutches would snag the saddle. It did not enter his mind that the years of flow had worn the walls to a smooth finish.

This latest scramble for life was not his most dangerous outing of all.

Not yet, it wasn't.

The past week or so flooded his mind with a series of images and head-photos of one Barney 'Tricky Finger' MacDill, killer from out-of-site, killer from darkness, killer from the back sides of barns, killer of several bank employees, killer of two sheriffs and who-knows-how-many deputies since his breakout two years earlier from the territorial prison of Montana. It was like Tricky Finger MacDill was a gang on his own, everywhere at once, fear in any and all kinds of towns and settlements that made up Montana where he might suddenly appear, bent on new crimes of irreparable odds, uncountable riches.

Where would such a man get to spend, in any kind of comfort, the masses of ill-gotten coin and currency that had been twisted to his coffers? Gardenhire figured it would never happen; and thus, it said his life, as well as that of his prey, were never going to change until death or final incarceration, one or the other: he preferred the other but left the choice unstated; no sense messing things up.

It was MacDill's fashion, so given over by evidence, to alarm as many people as he could in the widest areas and in the shortest time: it would all spur his drive for funds he'd never get to spend, all that stash he kept hidden in a place unknown to anybody else, most likely. Such men as MacDill do not have friends that can be trusted, like a bullet in the back can take care of that kind of problem.

The sudden thought of erosion of river banks and walls, making them too smooth to snag even a rugged saddle on the move, made Gardenhire think that he might become a saddle thief himself grabbing off the first one that came his way, that might be found in his path.

And so, it was that he came upon a horse, saddle and all, tethered to a clump of brush in a wooded area, the smoky remnants of a fire caught on the edge of the day.

The horse snickered its recognition of an intruder and the prone figure at rest on a ground blanket leaped to alert, a pistol in hand as he rolled over in place and came to his knees. He appeared to be a most ordinary man but was clean-shaven and totally bald, not a hair on his head. Those quickly-gleaned observations caused Gardenhire but momentary concern, yet a sort of awe began to revolve in his mind, and made him blurt out, "What the hell happened to all your hair?"

The strange bald man, perhaps in his mid-twenties, replied, "What the hell happened to your saddle? Why are you riding without a saddle in this kind of country?"

His perplexity was honest and sincere.

Gardenhire held up his hands and said, "Sorry to spoil your sleep, sorry to give you such a start, but I lost my saddle in the river and have to get around half a mountain to retrieve it and get back on the chase for a killer on the loose. You best be aware he's loose hereabouts, and he'll shoot before he asks your name."

"Who are you?" came the retort.

"I'm Sheriff Greg Gardenhire, from the Territorial Offices, all counties, of this here piece of Montana. I have to warn you again, if this dude I'm after came on you like I did, you'd be dead now. He'd have shot you before you woke up, before your horse had a chance to snicker his alert.

"Oh, okay, Sheriff. I'm Garvy Grant, lately of Pointed Hill, a good day and a half ride back toward the Idaho border. I guess you want an answer about my hair." A definite loss of stature seemed to crush him.

His shoulders went into an immediate droop, just as if his personality had undergone a soulful change. "I went to sleep drunk as hell with my wife irate as she's ever been and in my drunken sleep she cut off every bit of my hair, down there too," whereon he had pointed to his crotch, "and then she bolted with the gent she had been cheating on me with. Who knows where they are now and who cares, and I'm out here in the woods waiting for my hair to grow back. I figure that'll be somewhere around a month of waiting and I'll have to hunt down food and keep away from people and you show up, a sheriff without a saddle and hunting down a bad dude."

Gardenhire laughed a hearty laugh, and said," Ain't we the odd pair. Here's me, a sheriff, without a saddle, on the hunt for a real bad dude, and you got no hair."

Their joint laughter could have wakened any sleeping body in a mile, and they ended up almost in a jig, just about dancing around the remnants of the fire, until Gardenhire came to a quick stop and said, "I'm gonna need your saddle, Garvy. I'll give you a signed paper for what it's worth if I manage to lose this one too, that the territory will make good,

7

on my sworn word, but you'll also be a man without a saddle and with no hair for your own while."

The sheriff's smile was a yard wide, and the bald man said, "Think I should stay right here, Greg?"

"What I'd do if I was you is to leave this place just like it is, including the remnant type of smoky ash fire, but move your sleeping spot back into deeper woods, only as far as you can spot anybody prowling real close to here."

They shook hands after the sheriff saddled his horse with the bald man's saddle, Garvy Grant saying, "You go find your killer, Sheriff, and your saddle, which ever comes first, and I'll grow a hair or two wherever it finds a good spot."

They enjoyed another laugh at their peculiar difficulties, Grant checking himself in a ludicrous manner, and adding, "I don't know where I'd want it first." He had one hand tucked inside his beltline.

Their parting, unlike most partings, was joyful both ways.

In two days, Gardenhire found his saddle nudged against the river banking after he had ridden around the mountain, and let it dry out against a rock face heated by the sun. The next day, sitting the damp saddle and with the second saddle toted behind him, he found the last known path of Barney 'Tricky Finger' MacDill where he had left it. He crossed the river at another spot and came back over it, as it headed where he hoped it wouldn't go, toward the high forest where Garvy Grant was hopefully growing hair.

The longer he followed the same general direction, the more he figured, intuition kicking in its final chips, that there'd be a calamitous encounter along the line. Several times, even in deep studies, he heard the laughter of Garvy Grant, saw his bald head catching the sun with unknown reflections making their loose ways in every conceivable direction, thinking how he could not see what had disappeared on his body.

The sheriff became more suspect of every bend or turn in the trail, sometimes working his way around a certain point looking for easy-to-see sniping sites along the way, in the bald overheads of rocky outcroppings, from the edge of a huge tree wide in places like a barn, almost locked in the clutter of thick bushes, groups of young saplings and seedlings like they were hanging out together.

Then, at one turn in the trail, the line of sight from many mountainous places as clear as could be wanted, he heard from some distant point the shot of a rifle, or the echo of such a shot. His worry was of his hairless, wifeless, saddleless friend alone in the wilderness with a most serious and instant killer on the loose.

There was but the one shot or the one echo; no second shot or echo sounded, no return fire from one fired upon. The worst of signs and possibilities came upon him, so that he spurred his mount to get where the action had taken place. "Damned fool bald-headed kid getting caught unawares," sounded alive in his mouth. "I best hurry to check the damage."

He brushed aside the bush and brush of the trail, afraid at every turn of a sniper shot coming his way, of seeing his young friend spread wide open on the base of the trail, every hair due his head, due his chin, due his crotch, gone forever.

The silence coming his way was intolerance itself. It burned him. There had been so many good ways of it being a resplendent growth at some point in time.

He leaned in the saddle around one familiar turn and was joyously surprised to see Garvy Grant standing beside the remnants of a fire, soft and slowly-moving smoke emanating from dark logs in a pile of embers before they would fall apart into nothing more than ashes.

Serenity abounded.

He could not believe it, the scene in front of him.

The hairless one was still hairless, the sun moving tracer-like across the dome of his head, throwing off miniature lightning strikes, his hands flung outward in a gesture of hopeless outcome.

All that Sheriff Gardenhire could say was, "I brought your saddle back just like I promised," and the bald one said, "I can't see anyplace else, but I got me some new hair growing that I can see, down here," and he had his hand inside his belt buckle.

They turned their dual surprise into laughter as Garvy Grant snuck a look down inside his pants and said, "At least I can see these ones here but none of anything else."

The laughter flooded the deep-woods forest, each one thinking of their own odd connections, the pluses and the minuses, the could-have beens and the maybe's everyone knows, until they had reached an unreachable point, when bald, wifeless, almost hairless Garvy Grant said, in the great surprise of the century, "and I got your killer too."

He walked slowly away from the center of the fire, stood where the sheriff told him he should be on watch, turned a bit proudly it might be said, to the small pile of leaves at the edge of the clearing, scraped the thin, top layer aside, to show the one and only, the now dead, Barney 'Tricky Finger' MacDill, as still as he'd ever be, his unfired pistol still, real still, still in one hand.

That part of Montana, perhaps in all the Montana Territory, has never heard again the tumult, the gaiety, the congruence of such two-voiced laughter, even one more time, so help me Hannah.

Jack Barclay, foreman from Jell's Hill Ranch, was still in command of the crew at The Devil Crow's Saloon in the makeshift town of Porter Hill, Texas and they were talking about the only missing member of the outfit, Shag Hannah. Jack had offered his bit in the conversation: "That birthmark on Shag's face is so ugly spit won't hurt it, but makes ladies weak and plain sorrowful, not just the ones working here, but all over, ladies be damned. It ain't that he cries about it messing him up but wears it like a damned badge of honor. I guess, when you get right down to it, that's what it is, a badge of honor for lady counting, but still ugly as sin."

The crew of riders from Jell's Hill ranch were celebrating the last drive for a while, some of them surely to be let go until the next ride, a few held over for general work, and a few of them ready to ride over the horizon and never be seen again, just the way Texas was exploding under their hooves, cattle carrying the territory on its back nearly half a century after the savage Alamo loss at the hands of the eventual leg man himself, Santa Anna, Mexico's part-time savior, politician, general, the *Napoleon wanna-be* of those times.

One cowpoke, sombrero at an odd angle on his head, already leaning against the wall in one corner, yelled out, "Where's Shag now, Jack? He still at the ranch?" Innuendo leaped across the room from a slurred mouth.

Shag Hannah, the ladies man, was the only one of the crew who hadn't shown up at the saloon.

The question from the corner might well have said, "Is he still back there with the boss?" who was the widow, Sarah Jell, 30 ought-something nobody knew for certain, gorgeous from sun-up to sun-down, and then more perfect than any of them could imagine, including Jack Barclay himself. He was at least two years in love with her, or dreaming about her, if he bothered counting the days, the weeks, the months of a one-sided entanglement with a gifted horse rider, a beauty in the saddle the way her golden hair grabbed more than a fair share of the sun, starter and closer of dozens of dreams on a daily or nightly occurrence.

"He waiting for nighttime, Jack?" came from the end of the bar, which could have come from any one of the crew.

"Shag don't wait nothing, including dark of night," came another herder volunteer, third or fourth or fifth beer in a hurry jumping ahead of himself, the way some men can pass a whole day in one short afternoon at the rail or close enough to it.

"Wish I had some more of him in me, or on me," said a mostly quiet cowpoke in one corner, who was almost jumped on immediately by a cohort clear across the room, waving his hand in the air, as if he had to make known to all parties his own grasp of the last comment.

"You got one o' them birthmarks on you, Kurt, that you never showed us. Not even at the river washing off the long ride we took on our time getting here?" He looked around the room as though he was expecting the women to pop up. His laughter at himself caught up the whole saloon full of cowpokes, and the laughter grew into a huge ball sounding like a giant at his joy.

Another ranch hand, after a sudden silence, added his bit of quandary; "What I want to know is it mush, mash or magic old Shag's toting around? I can't see none of it, so I don't know what to believe. Are you gents just egging on some of us dumbbells in the crowd? Appears to me we're building somethin' out of nothin'." He drained off his half glass of beer and shot the empty down along the bar to the barkeep, all hands of the rail-benders raised in salute.

Jack Barclay whispered to a confidante at his table, "All of them, they're all in the dark about what Shag really is, and you can take it from me that he's one helluva ranch hand, knows the trail's do's and don'ts and all the other stuff as well as me and I'd put him up against anybody in this room," he paused to accentuate *anybody,* "including you and me, in a gunfight, quick draw and straight on face to face."

"Hell, Jack," came the reply also in a whisper, "I ain't ever seen him shoot a damned gun for all that's worth. But I wouldn't doubt a word you can say in the matter, not a single word. I been ridin' with you seems forever and never heard you tell a lie. You never steered me wrong even once that I know of, old *straight arrow* himself."

At that same moment the good words were being spread around The Devil Crow's Saloon, Shag Hannah and Sarah Jell were bound with ropes and were lying side by side in a small room at the Jell's Hill ranch house after being surprised, having coffee in the kitchen, by four masked bandits, each one of the bandits taking turns yelling loudly, screaming orders, binding and knotting ropes in place on their hands and feet, and shoving them into the small utility room, wooded plugs knocked into rows along two walls and used for visitors' duds, and odd lots of odds and ends..

"You recognize any of them, Shag?" Sarah Jell was still the boss, and glad they hadn't tied a bandana over her mouth. "One voice I know I heard before, but I just can't find a face for it. I'll kick myself once I find out and we certainly will get out of this scrape one way or another. The others have never been here. I've never heard their voices before and I'm positive of that."

The nod of her heard was affirmation he had seen before, as it seemed to say, "Now you've heard me, so we understand each other." She was still the boss, her husband, Harland Jell, gone almost five years, her never losing stride while running the ranch. Not for a second.

"They're new to me, at least I think they are," Shag said, as he tussled with the ropes on his wrists first, then at his ankles. He winked at Sarah, smiled, felt a crease on the birthmark exaggerate its presence, widen. It always happened when he smiled, like odds were being deployed, brought into the argument, arrangements on the make. Early on he had learned the differences brought into play.

A loud yell came from somewhere in the house, "Look what the hell I found in here! Place must be loaded with it. Let's get her out here and drag it out of her. Could be a damned goldmine on our hands."

Another voice, thicker, deeper, trying to be muffled thought Shag, said, "Keep quiet. I told you a dozen times, keep your mouth shut." An immediate silence sat motionless, breathless.

Shag nodded at Sarah again. "Most likely that bigmouth has been here before, but it must have been before I came here."

"I still can't find a face to go with any including the last two voices. It's obvious they've taken off the masks or at least loosened them up while out of our sight, which means they're afraid of being recognized later on if there is a later on, or we can identify them to the law sooner than later."

Shag shuffled his hands, squirmed and wiggled around in a search for a rough edge, found it, and began working a wrist knot against a bumpy knot on a rough wall log, smiled at her again, came taut as he heard steps outside the room. He was still, silent, his eyes shut resisting a reaction, his chin resting on his chest in a defeated manner, when the door was snapped open.

A masked man looked in, his eyes showing an aqua shade through the mask eye slits, and closed the door quickly.

"That was damned quick of you, Shag. Fooled me like it did him." Sarah's head swayed. "At least, I hope it did. I'll be owing you if it turns out well."

Shag, knowing change even before it happened, added, "I can feel the goodness already, I swear." The knot on his wrist was looser and he worked slowly, surely against a selected edge, thinking of a knife being at work. To get his feet free, he had to free his hands.

He asked Sarah, "Say, girl, you think you got any guns in here?" He almost kissed her when she nodded, smiled, and replied, "Harland was a stickler for protection. I thought when one of them out there screamed that he'd found one of the guns. Harland hid them around the house, on top of beams, in tight spaces no one'd check out in a hundred years, like in that corner behind you, right behind that old wooden carving of the ranch brand, a pistol's stuck in the hollow backside, primed and loaded.

Her smile was a yard wide and her lips pursed with a quick promise. "Have at 'em when you get ready, and we'll talk turkey later." She hadn't once looked at the birthmark sitting on his face bold as some wounds appear from old near soul-deep damage.

One word came from Shag's mouth as he said, "Ah," as resolute as a salute, and he swung free one hand and then his other hand, then undid the knots at his ankles, put his fingers across his lips to ensure silence from Sarah, and found the pistol behind the old brand carving. It looked, to Sarah, mighty comfortable in his hand.

When the door opened, a masked bandit stepped in and saw Sarah still bound on the floor and felt a pistol horseshoe-hard against his neck. His mouth dropped open at the lower part of the mask, but not a word escaped him. In one swipe, Shag ripped the mask off, didn't recognize him, but pointed down to Sarah and whispered, "Untie her or you're dead." His tone was harsh, and loaded with evil at the ready, a finger taut at the trigger, the pistol steady as a ramrod.

And Shag Hannah soon had two pistols in his hands as he heard heavy steps coming across the outer room, and a voice saying, "What the hell's going on in there?"

In one quick move, Shag dove into the outer room and from a horizontal position on the floor shot dead the heavy man who fell in a heap mere feet away from him, a single gurgle leaking from his mouth.

Scrambling sounds emanated from elsewhere in the house, accompanied by a shout, "Shag's loose. Let's get the hell outta here."

"Let 'em go," Shag said to Sarah, her eyes wide and blue in wonder and surprise, "we can nab them easy later on. We better clean up in here and get down to the real important stuff."

Sarah Jell, widow, ranch owner, felt warm for the first time in hours, in years.

False dawn's first signal slipped into the trail-end town of Bountiful, Kansas, the cattle drive over a few days earlier, the train loaded and gone, some cowpokes from the drive hanging on for a few more laughs, a few more drinks, a last look at someone special, before they had to light out for a new drive, cows, dust, work galore on top of work, lousy food some days, thirst, sore rumps, campfire camaraderie, ballads with a guitar to fall asleep with, dreams of another life.

There floated on the air a tinkle from a sick piano, or a player who wasn't a player, a tinkerer, caught up in dawn's reality, only another drive sitting in the wings of his life waiting to happen, be something to do.

Sheriff Spade Pickett heard the late night (or early morning) tinkle from the piano in the Bull's Head Saloon directly across the street from his room at Martha Henry's Boarding House. It was plaintive, as sad as hope might be, or might get this late in the night, this early in the day. Courses in live events came back from New Hampshire cities such as Concord and Keene amongst other places he'd worked, and even little towns like Gilsum had their share of bad luck, to his good luck.

His training in New Hampshire, back along the trail, paid handsome dividends in a new setting, as long as his eyes and ears were wide open. And *Live Free or Die*, NH's motto, seemed as valid as ever out here on the trail. The start for him was as a newsboy on home deliveries, but studying every murder case, sending his thirst and hunger for tracking killers and evil sorts onto legal training through an old neighborhood constable. The training stuck in place, his constable's badge in his saddle bag when he rode out of Gilsum, New Hampshire for the last time, heading west.

Now, on this night, he thought about his past as his deputy, Morgan Pulver, was most likely sleeping soundly, a hangover coming up with its kick probably an hour away yet, the bunk in the jail more comfortable than many sleeping spots on this particular morning, and one rabble-rousing cowpoke in a cell from a serious altercation, but his opponent from the dispute of gunfire unknown to this point.

Pickett spoke to the walls, as was a morning custom, as if rehearsing his day to come, what he might expect of it: Pulver would wake up with the dull ache in his head, a matter of a few hours before he'd be tip-top again, ready for a lazy day in the town, or all the action a town could bring his way.

Pickett liked him except for his tussle with the drink, a nightly thing, though he'd be ready for a long ride of a posse, or a day on guard in the jail, whatever the sheriff wanted of him.

With his face washed in the bowl on the small bureau in his room, hands free of a night's sleep, ready for a meal at Martha's bidding, the long-time sheriff of Bountiful donned his pants, socks, and boots, put on a clean shirt Martha left hanging on the door every day. With care, he put on his gun belt, checked the cylinders of his two pistols, adjusted his mind and frame for whatever the day would bring his way.

Martha made the start of his day easy, with fresh water in the bowl, a clean shirt, and good meal.

Morgan Pulver made it as bad as it could get.

He knocked twice at the door of his office, the jail attached. One way in, one way out, in full view of the town, sitting beside the bank, diagonally across from the saloon, just down the street from Martha's place.

Pulver did not respond. Pickett knocked again. And again. No answer.

"Must be a beauty he tied on," Pickett said to the morning and himself, alone at the moment.

He dug for his key in the junk in his pocket, found it, opened the door.

Murder was the scene in front of him: Morgan Pulver, bloody as hell, flat on the floor, part of the bunk atop him, posse rifles torn from the wall rack and littering the floor like dead logs. Blood was all over the floor and the walls. The prisoner was dead in his cell, a rope around his neck and hanging from the bars of the one window in the jail.

A broken bottle of booze littered the cell floor. Another bottle's remnants were scattered on the office floor. The three chairs in the office were broken in pieces and the pieces were strewn about the room.

The most salient thing in the room other than death itself was the smell of booze, old booze, heaved booze, sickness on its own.

Just about everything in the room was smashed or upset or tossed about as if a wind or a tornado had rushed through, or whirled in the room like a dervish, and escaped out the lone window between the bars ... the way it must have come in.

Everything was tossed but the heavy desk that was the main piece of furniture in the room. That was as rigid as ever, solid oak, a sign of durability, of permanence. It made Pickett think of death and separation and loneliness and the loss of a friend, likeable but troublesome, who lay dead at his feet, beat all to hell. Memories that would outlast even the solid oak desk.

At the door, he looked back and took the contents and the conditions in the room right into the depths of his mind. He yelled to a passerby, "Go get Doc Randolph for me and Hickory over at the saloon. I need them right away."

The three men gathered in the midst of the mess.

Doc Randolph said, "Morg was beat with something heavy, blunt, but nothing like anything in the room. It was carried off, but it must have been heavy, or big. I can't see how it was carried out and through the town, no matter what time it was. Cowpokes were all over the town last night."

He looked at the sheriff and said, "The door was locked, Spade? Tight as the old drum?"

"I knocked a few times, then louder, and nothing. I had to dig the key out of my pants pocket. Never had to do that before, Morg always opening up though he was hung over. You know how he was. Hell, I miss that boy already."

Dell Hickory, owner of the saloon, said, "It sure as hell sits kind of impossible with me, Spade. The door must have been opened and shut, then locked by someone with a key. How many keys?"

Pickett said, "Mine, which was in my pocket, and the one for the office, and it's still in the desk where it's always been. That desk ain't been touched."

The three men looked again around the office, taking in all they could, and the doc said, "I'll take care of Morg if you got nothing else coming out of him, Spade, but you got a mystery on your hand I can't help any more than I have. I'll get some boys and get him out of here."

He turned with the most quizzical look on his face, looked at the office again, peered into the cell, and said, "I'll take care of him too." He pointed at the murdered prisoner, dead in the cell, a rope around his neck. "Looks like a serious party took place here last night." He walked out and into the new day.

Hickory, watching as the doctor left, said, "Spade, it sure looks like someone had it in for Morg," then he tipped his head and looked at the dead prisoner, and added, "or him, and Morg got in the way of it all."

He shook his head as the doc had done, looked at the door, then at the one barred window, at the mess all about the entire jail. "Anybody mad at you, Spade? Anybody serious like? Dumps a lot on you, you know. Your office, your deputy, your prisoner. You having the only key that could lock the door. Don't look nice at all."

With an immediate qualification, he said, "Hell, I know it ain't your style, ain't your way at all, Spade, but it will sell some of the wagging tongues that always come around like clothesline stuff when the law gets questions on itself. You got any ideas?"

Pickett shook his head. "It was not quick, this whole thing," he said. "It was some time in the making. I feel positive of that."

"How do you figure that, Spade?"

"Well, the booze got in here. Morg never had a jug in here before, or a bottle even. Never once, and he's been drunk before, a dozen times."

"So?"

"I think it came in through the window in the cell. The prisoner got drunk, Morg saw it eventually, perhaps joined in, got drunker himself."

Hickory said, "Think the prisoner killed Morg and then locked himself back in the cell? But the cell key is on the hook over there on the wall."

"Then who killed the prisoner? Who hung him on the bars? He commit suicide?"

"That's what it looks like to me," Hickory cracked quickly. "Just like that." The light of sudden resolution was in his eyes like a lamp had been lit.

"How'd the door get locked from the outside?" the sheriff said, still studying the room. He thought and answered himself, "Unless it was never unlocked after I locked it when I left last night, Morg asleep on the cot, the town almost on its last legs, me heading for Martha's and a nightcap with her, and the key in my pocket."

"It only locks with a key from the outside?"

"Yes," Pickett said. "It gets locked from the inside with a twist of the little stopper there." He pointed at the little gizmo on the face of the lock. The way they made the lock, like the gent who made the cell lock made the door lock too, almost in the same way, but no gizmo on the cell lock. Once I lock the door from the outside, only a key opens the door from the outside but anyone on the inside can unlock it."

"The cell door locks with a key?" Hickory was full of questions.

"Yup," Pickett replied. "And the key's still hanging there on the wall."

Hickory showed puzzle anew on his face. I can't offer much more, Spade. I'll have to be going to start the day at the saloon. Takes a lot to get it on the road."

He saw a new twist on the sheriff's face as the sheriff said, "You've been here a lot longer than me, Dell. Who built your place?"

Quizzically Dell Hickory answered, "Why Claude Auger, and he built the bank and I'm pretty sure he built the jail too. He had a lot of projects going at one time."

"Did them in a hurry, too, did he?"

Hickory said, "I realize that in the winter when the place gets cold as hell for a while. I put down some rugs under the poker tables and along the bar, but they get ripped to hell after a while. Keeps the feet a bit warmer in the winter, though. Why'd you ask?" He was staring at the sheriff in another quandary.

"Whoever did this sure didn't come in the door, didn't come down through the roof, but could have come up from underneath here." He stomped on the floor, hoping to feel a loose board.

"You wait here until you hear from me."

Spade Pickett, sheriff of Bountiful, left his office, walked to the side of the building, got down on hands and knees and saw the marks in the ground where someone dragged himself, and dragged something behind him. The marks were easy for a trail reader to read, a posse scout, Pickett with several years at that task. They lead him to his last suspicion, where he found several floor boards of his office gripped to beams with a strange clamp, twisted tight as one could manage with his fingers. Three of the boards were no more than four feet long.

With a quick twist he loosed all the clamps, pushed up on one board, which came easily free from the beams it spanned and he stuck his head up into the office, on one side of the desk which had not been moved, the only piece of furniture in the office that had not been moved.

He had accomplished the maneuver soundlessly, and said in a light voice, near a whisper, "Dell, can you hear me?"

"Where the hell are you, Spade?" Hickory said, unable to see over the desk to where the sheriff stuck his head up through the opening in the floor.

Another board was moved out of the way, and Pickett pushed himself off the ground and up into his office, to where an amazed Dell Hickory watched him rise as like a ghost from the nether world beneath them.

"Now we got some answers, Dell," Pickett said, and let me tell you something else … check under your own building for what I'll tell you I found under here, and there's the same thing under the bank next door. I'm thinking that whoever did Morg in and the prisoner and would get away with it, they'd think about your place and the bank in the dead of night, and be done with each one of them too."

Hickory was amazed, to a point, and said, "That damned Auger had this set in place for his big payday, didn't he?"

With another look on his face, the sheriff said, "We can't prove it, Dell, but we sure can set it up for the next try, which would likely be at your place, and after a drive is over and lots of cash from a few big nights is on hand, but we have to plan it, like he's planning it on his end, only we feed him the right bait."

So it went for a few weeks, an unknown killer had beat the hell out of a deputy in his own jail, killed a prisoner who might have seen it all, and got away with it free as a lark on the prairie.

Some townsfolk laughed about Spade Pickett and his plight.

But it didn't take long for more action of the same kind.

Another cattle drive, almost 10,000 head, came up the trail from Texas, with a large crew on hand, and they broke loose for a few nights, with Dell Hickory exclaiming loudly, "These are the best nights we've ever had in the Bull's Head Saloon, the best nights ever."

The salon was shut down at 2 A.M. on a fateful day, the last drunken patron escorted from the door at that time, the lights doused, the doors locked, and the light in Dell Hickory's room thumbed out just after 3.A.M.

It was just before 4 A.M. when Sheriff Spade Pickett and saloon owner Dell Hickory, in their stocking feet, free of boots, sitting quiet as possums with blankets under their feet, heard the sounds under the floor some 20 feet away, in a corner of the room.

Every lamp in the saloon had been turned off, darkness sat across the room dense as a cloud, and the simple noise of a few metallic snaps echoed upward from the floor. A sound like that of a board sliding on another wooden surface came audible. It sounded like a whisper to the two men sitting still as night owls, their pistols lying on a blanket draped over the table.

Pickett held up his empty hand in front of Hickory's face, suggesting silence, patience.

Neither man moved, their breaths coming as muted as possible, only the threat of a sneeze or a cough hanging in the air to mess things up. Then came the whisper of another board sliding on a wooden surface, followed by the slight gasp of a man at labor, and Claude Auger rose up in the darkness as strange as any apparition ever seen in the Bull's Head Saloon.

Only when Auger was fully erect and had stepped away from the hole in the floor, did he feel the gun in his back, and the words of Sheriff Spade Pickett say, "You're under arrest for the murder of Deputy Morgan Pulver, Bountiful prisoner Lucas Wilbur, breaking and entry in the early dawn of the Bull's Head Saloon, and the planned robbery of the Bountiful Bank. Nice work, Auger … if you could get it done."

It was all over but the hanging.

In Chicago in 1861, before the great war in the states started, before she had a chance to go further west, Maud Wilkesbarn thought things over, including what might be in front of her, and changed her family name, legal or not, from Wilkesbarn to Maverick. She kept the "Maud" in place because she'd swear to the day of her death she could hear her mother announcing her to potential babysitters, strangers, old friends dropping by, or new men she might be interested in, as "This sweetheart is my Maud."

She was 21 years old as we start here, svelte, smooth as dreams in her attire, understood men's glances without knowing the cause in her invaluable attribute of being chaste, though some unknown connection was working within.

To her ultimate surprise, she woke up one morning in love. One man among all men had appeared at the gray edges of her night, the silence about him broken by the soft murmur of a lullaby coming her way from early life, its words gone but the hum of it a near bit of silence, faint but audible, as much magic as not.

His name was Devon Hartnet, about twice as old as her, coming full of energy, his own dreams, and a plan to bring it home, as he put it, knowing she was at ear shot. She had looked at him once or twice as he spoke, evoked another mere plan in his mind, of capturing her for good, young as she was, older as he was, time and age not to be quibbled with, not for a second.

His pursuit showed her slow to move away, but moving toward him faster than he did with his great plans, to announce to him outright that she was in love with him from first sight. They, as a result of her fast maneuvers, were married, and he said, as if she had already dreamed of it, "We're going west to build an empire, a massive one, one we can be proud of, a whole valley of our own that I can see with my eyes closed."

She closed her eyes and said, "I can see it, too." He thought he could not love her no more than he did at the moment, but he did.

Each one thought they were the perfect couple at the beginning of a grand life, of goods and gratuities, of grace and grandness.

They ended up in one of the 7 territories that would comprise Montana Territory before it was to become a state much later, in 1889, long after the Sioux and Cheyenne tribes won the huge battle of the Little Big Horn in 1876, long after the army forces constituted a new territorial control that guaranteed their valley interests, now huge and cumbersome, were vested in his name.

All seemed well and good until the day a wild horse kicked Devon in the head. Maud had him put down in a favored place, high on a mount looking down on most of his assets, now hers without a doubt, old Chicago still known to her and old visions.

She went to work to increase her gain, driven by desires her mother had known and were being carried through to a sound reality, saying time after time, "If you're going to want something, make sure it's big and strong. Maud's grasp on her chunk of the territory was sure-fisted, and looked always to be getting bigger and stronger.

The Hartnet spread, called by many as *Two Aitches (HHs)*, employed two dozen men, a *big house* cook, a kitchen mother, a pair of maids that worked kitchen to bedroom, a foreman, Gil Bentry, who needed no house key, and enough of the hired hands had come as army veterans of combat in the territories.

But Maud Hartnet kept her eyes open for a new *mister special* to make his appearance, sweep her into another piece of heaven, as she said to one of the maids, Alspeth Stiperd, a 20-year old beauty who could not keep her own door locked. It was she who told Maud one day that her new man, Maud's new man, had come looking for work. "He looks special all the way," she said with a wink.

As it turned out, Finn McMorrin had been hired by Gil Bentry. McMorrin struck him as rugged, honest, experienced, handsome as a warrior without paint, a young man of 30 bound for good graces about the place. Destiny had already worked for him, but a sure story followed him in his tracks, perhaps on his trail.

When Maud asked Bentry about the new hire, she got the protective speech. "He's so good looking, Maud, that there has to be a story in his saddlebag. Guys that good looking always have a hunk of garbage somewhere in their immediate past, but I got nothing out of him. Your try at it might be better, but he's a worker, I can tell you that, and seems dedicated. Would swear to loyalty, earn his keep, keep his eyes open. Know what I mean?"

Maud kept watch on Finn McMorrin, felt the old issues moving inside, had to make a move, and decided a direct one, again, would be best for her, and him.

She corralled him near the largest barn one day, admired again his looks, the handsome looks, the structural strength, the span of shoulders, the slim hips, the light in his eyes that turned on and off at intervals, saying things in his own way.

"I will tell you, Finn McMorrin, if that's your name, that Maud Hartnet is not legally my name, not from the first minute. I also dropped much of my past coming to where I am now, and I suspect that you, as handsome a dog as I've ever seen, has a past and perhaps another name you're hiding behind, as I am. I, in fact, may still be Maud Wilkesbarn as far as I know, a name that really bothered me when I toted it around. I didn't even like the sound of it or whatever or wherever it came from or what it might mean."

She thought she had been opened wide enough and managed a half laugh as appropriate punctuation.

He felt her hand reach out and touch his arm, as if to send along both an excuse and a confirmation of trust for both of them. His comfort zone reacted to the simple touch, which they each recognized, accepted, knew was an overture in the making.

Her unmasking of events, the exposé of her life, continued: "The legal paper trail went astray a long time ago. The fact that we're dealing with territories and laws and rules of order that may or will raise their ugly heads as development comes with them, does not cause me any fear or desperation. The fact of all matters will one day become history in the books that will legislate our lives, our property rights, our past histories. Like dreams, lies, untruths, will become facts in books, in registers, in history. Those people among us who will manipulate rules and orders for their own good, must also attend to what we as individuals need to make our way out here in the territories."

She had crossed many thresholds in her openness, thrown light on life itself, caused history to blossom on the spot.

She paused, then asked, "Does that loosen you up, Finn McMorrin?"

Her eyes had lit up, he saw. The old connections were at work, and a sense of comfort and acceptance had been found. His boots were on solid ground, the shadow of the barn had lifted, the sun shone overhead. Good signs for a man. This was no dream. This was really happening. Time of the past seemed to be swallowed up in the new feelings that worked inside his frame. He felt new, relieved, some bridge or span had been crossed in just a matter of minutes. Amazement leaped in the air.

His hand reached out to touch her hand, even before he replied. "It sure does, Ma'am, trusting all that to me, just a trail hand who lucked out on getting a job here. Might be the best thing ever happened to me." The blue light, she noticed, was in his eyes, too.

"So," she said, "You can tell me the whole past you're carrying around, and it will go no further than me, as I have promised."

"The fact is that I killed two men who killed my mother and my wife. I would have let justice, if it had a fair appearance, do its thing but the two men were from a huge spread with dozens of pals who'd swear by them, tell lies for them, beat the crimes in court. It had happened before with the same group. I couldn't let it happen again. I'll admit it was bad enough thinking about my mother, but they messed with my wife before they killed her. That crushed me. I caught up with them and I shot both of them right in the head and left it all behind me and my real name of ..."

She shushed him with a finger touch on his lips, to hold back, as if forever, his true name, and said, "They messed with your wife? I'm damned sorry to hear that and happy you got your revenge. We can go up to the house now, if it'd be okay with you, and have a coffee or a tea, whatever pleases you. We should be better acquainted."

There was no sound, no blast of light, no sky lit up, at the moment, but changes had occurred.

Life, as it was, was in transition for two obviously nameless souls, or two souls who'd have to learn new ways to address each other, which did not present any problem.

Bergund Columnard, from Shropshire, England, was reflecting on the trail he had used getting to this place in the absolute middle of nowhere in Hell and hoped to be outbound from there. He was, fact up front, in the Southwestern part of the United States, and bound by hot sands; lots of sand every which way he could see.

It was Columnard's second year of travel, 1873, after landing in Boston pointing his nose west after arrival, and after a sweep of local interests. Every once in a while, on the move, he allowed himself a bit of memory of the old country, how pieces kept sticking to him, and new memories coming along with those instant reflections, all wanting to be known again. It was as simple as that, wanting to be known again... as if he were the sole reservoir of Shropshire memories.

First off, he was a student of many corners and turns of the world, in and out of the classrooms, and then, second, he was a traveler, toting classroom knowledge with him, hungry for the next view just on or over the horizon, how its impact might knock him silly some days, explosive with joy, satisfaction, a new class of wonder working him into a newest frenzy.

Never-the-less, he loved the old history that had made the journey with him, all the way to this very damnable spot in the ass-end of a desert. He'd come out of Shropshire long after his studies were done at the knee of his grandfather, getting to know all the data of Shropshire being established during the division of Saxon Mercia into shires back in the 10th century. It was first mentioned in 1006 when, after the Norman Conquest, it experienced significant development, following favorable granting of some principal estates of the county to the most eminent of the Norman lords, and that included the horror who was Lord Hurlbert the Hungry, stabbed by a tree limb fallen onto his tent in a storm; the story being his son hung the first local he saw with an ax in his hands, perhaps the actual harbinger of the Shropshire Lad by the poet/writer A. E. Housman who was yet to write his words about young men and old life.

The Coalbrookdale area of his county was designated "the birthplace of the Industrial Revolution," due to significant technological developments that happened there, specifically construction of the first Iron Bridge which crossed the River Severn in Shropshire. Opened in 1781, the bridge was the first major one in the world to be made of cast iron. Bridges, since then, have continued the longer spans and the higher rises within many parts of the world.

The stories his grandfather told him about the bridge were magnificent memories from a man who worked as part of the labor force erecting the bridge, the first of the ironworkers soon to span the world, almost 100 years before Bergund was born.

Two further days of hellish travel, his horse dead behind him beside a wind-swept dune, he peaked another high dune and spotted the gift of a tree line, sparse at first, but thickening with closer sight. He found water, a small camp of miners on the move, managed to buy a horse, and continue his travels.

He didn't know where he was headed, except for one miner's advising him, "Due northwest is a town called Peak's Bend, not big, but can be a new starting point to wherever, and a sure exit from Hell, take it from me." He thought there was a double-twist of humor in the miner's expression, but held back his laughter.

Peak's Bend proved to be a godsend for Bergund, with his telling stories to small groups of folks, finding a lovely-looking widow whose husband had fallen dead on the trail a few months earlier and her needing a new second driver for her wagon. They coupled well and were on the trail further northwest a week later.

The train was composed of Conestoga wagons, Prairie Schooners, and a few odd vessels of the road, and they measured from 13 feet to 24-26 feet long at the bottom of the box, stood just over 3 feet off the ground and had wheels about 3 ½ feet in diameter. They were lumbering giants.

Myrna Lafferty was her name, Irish to the bone, comely, warm as a southwest breeze, shapely new denims just produced by Jacob Davis and Levi Strauss announcing her conscious comfort, her saying to him after little deliberation, "As soon as I heard you weaving your stories, I knew you were the man for me. My poor grandfather, in the ground back in Tipperary, schooled us on stories that mesmerized us, their contents coming better than lessons. Taught us well. Made us love the languages he was able to use, whatever they were.

She'd murmured the word "love" like it was a promise or a potion on hand. It was merely days later that the wagon master, Jed Hayes, noticed the way Bergund walked about, chest puffed a bit, congenial to all parties, a smile on his face, his world turned around. The wagon master merely nodded, a questionable wagon for the on-going journey was now squared away and in good hands.

Besides his story telling, familiarity with music and poetry, a bit of play acting, Bergund carried the ideas of the new industrial technology that had bloomed from various succeeding levels of the Abraham Darby family, ingenious Quakers back home in Shropshire. They discovered the making of cast iron, with which the first iron bridge ever made crossed its 200-foot span over the Severn River back home in Coalbrookdale, Shropshire. He knew the old mixtures, properties, functions and features as they stayed with him: softening blocks of iron and steel under great heat, (like the great leather bellows set to blowing by a water-fed cogged wheel near as big as a house that he had seen at America's first iron works in Saugus, just north of his port of entry at Boston.) That's where he saw the raw materials and chemicals added to raise carbon levels to aid in the mix of iron, carbon, silicon, sulphur and manganese, limestone and coke (carbon) at great heat; the heat necessary to melt down ingredients, generated by forcing air into or onto a furnace-like fire bed.

He had stated that at some point of their journey, the wagon train members would be shown, and allowed to participate to a degree, in the making of some objects of cast iron, to last forever, as he promised, "Forever." He'd not told anyone that he saw a use for the trophy swords some travelers favored as souvenirs of the war that almost ruined a nation's dream, as well as some other useless articles people carried in their wagons.

The word "Forever," captured everybody in the wagon train, even as the train grew, even as Bergund's reputation grew.

But neither did he tell them that he was still searching for a method of generating sufficient heat to form casts; *that'd be the ticket to the show*!

Every time a topic or question of how and what and why came up on most any topic, Myrna's new man was able to bring cause and reason into the mix of the conversation, the true mid-earth truth about such things. It was like that at night, under their wagon, when the stars, the moon, the very heavens, came to them as she exalted him for his ways with her ways, *near the perfect couple* as some of the women said of them.

Bergund was becoming the main wagon train attachment, which by then had grown to 33 wagons for the way north to Oregon. Some of the late additions came from other wagon trains that had begun in the south after the Civil War was over, with wagon master Jed Hayes on his third trip west. *If he can do it, so can I,* was often whispered out of his earshot.

Thus, in the early part of 1874, the wagon train left Peak's Bend for a place in Oregon, with Jed Hayes advising everybody on the train that they might have to fend off Indian attacks, but also those from surprise raids by a group of well-armed, well-maintained, well-controlled gang of thieves bent on robbing a whole train of its better goods. "They like to steal one wagon, load it up, under gunpoint of course, with all attractive, expensive, salable goods they can carry off in one wagon, harder to track than two or more wagons taken by gun."

The warning was not wasted on Bergund Columnard, shortly falling asleep under their wagon with Myrna Lafferty, her head on his shoulder, her arm across his chest, the stars off to the north sending signals he would never ignore, his mind working well after sleep in the carriage of dreams that returned in his wakeful hours.

It was not long before the show might be presented, the cast iron show, for which he needed a cause and a place to generate sufficient heat. All he had to do was to tell his idea to one or two fellow travelers, in a soft voice, and it would spread the length of the train.

One opportunity was his saying, "We ought to make poles, in small round sections of cast iron, perhaps about 8 feet long, upon which when assembled will someday fly our flag in that place where we settle down with our forever dreams."

The word went the length of the wagon train and Bergund searched his dreams, saw the type of place he'd need, so when the cliffs at the edge of a mountain range almost spoke out to him, he knew the place again, the way it had come to him in a deep sleep and its dream carried far with him.

With help from others, he built with rocks a forge-like fireplace near the base of a cliff, including a hole at the back end of the fireplace by which he could pump air to brighten the fire, raise its heat level, melt iron and associated ingredients, which included the steel of 4 swords saved as souvenirs of the Great War, old iron pieces, coke, sulfur, phosphorus, and a few other raw materials he could find readily. From a rope slung overhead on a smooth ledge, he pulled and loosened the rope ends attached to a fan-like structure at the back of the forge. A new-world miracle in an old-world setting.

The flames flickered at impact, brightened, made quick promise of higher heat temperature.

After several tries, the materials melted and he poured the melt into sand bars for forming. The cast iron bars hardened into several pieces about 8-foot long, hard enough for "forever."

When the bars were cooled, he had them slung under his wagon, lengthwise, to haul to the final destination; for him and the others, it was a victory in the middle of nowhere, a victory of knowledge over simplicity, new world coming atop the old world in the least of celebrations.

There were no Indian raids thereafter, but one afternoon, the aforementioned gang of thieves caught them all unaware, searched with drawn weapons all wagons and piled all their loot in the Lafferty-Columnard large wagon, ready for an early morning run for the bushes.

All train people were ordered to their sleep by the thieves; "None of you are hurt. And we've done our bit. You can go your way once we leave you. You have been very receptive to us. Now go to sleep."

As it was, the chosen wagon was loaded to its brim with the loot, tied up with canvas at the tail end so nothing would fall out of the wagon. "Locked and loaded," as it might be said!

In the deep of night, storyteller, traveler, student of the ways of the world, Bergund Columnard, with the help of a new love of his life, slung a length of cast iron, due someday supposedly for a flag pole element, across the bottom side of the wagon box, between the two rear wheels of their wagon. It fit loosely but silently into place.

Prior to dawn, Bergund cautioned other folks to be gun-ready in the morning when things "get rumpled a bit."

"Up and at 'em, everybody," roared a bandit's voice too early for morning. "We're leaving with our new wagon, so just sit by. All is well."

The voice yelled another order, "Okay, Smokey, get 'em on the run. Hi ya, boy! Hi yah, boy! Hi yah!"

The Lafferty-Columnard wagon, a large Prairie Schooner, bigger than some plains' houses, lunged forward with their teams' initial draw and came to a noisy, metallic and deafening stop. The team could not budge the wagon another foot.

"Hi yah, I said! Hi yah!"

The wagon did not move, and wagon folks, now armed from secret sources, surrounded the band of bandits caught in a circle.

Bergund Columnard said, "It's a stand-still, boys. You were fair as far as thievery goes, but that's it. You all can go your way now just like we will. This wagon of ours is not going anyplace without us."

"From the first word, I swear," said Myrna Lafferty not much later, "I knew you were my new man."

She hugged him.

The shot had come down from the needle-like Nail Mountain, killing the second of Rico Belotti's sons in a month, and former sheriff Doyle Pickler, on the scene less than a month as temporary sheriff, was sure of a few things: "The shooter, a sniper first class, you gotta admit, was the killer, and he's been hiding out on Brother's Cliff since the night before at least."

"What makes you come up with that idea, Doyle? Could have been 50 cowpokes in there yesterday. We can't check out no 50 men. Hell, the whole Carvin crowd was there yesterday for Pate's birthday." Doyle's assistant, Jack Smitlyn, in the sheriff's estimation, was still learning how to breathe properly, or hold his breath at the right time. "No two ways about it," he might have erroneously muttered.

"That makes our job easier, Jackie boy, because they all came together from the ranch the other way down the Territory Road, every last one of them. Folks and yolks get caught in the same mix, often or not."

His father once said that to him, and the old man's ways had become part of his inheritance. "This shooter was in town yesterday and was out here ahead of us, and that was before last night came on us. No way he could have come from out of town and climbed up there in darkness. Don't think about it any other way. He'd have been dead on his own choice; fall, slip, jumpin' for a grip on a real bastard of a mountain which we all know," the voice cold as the steel of twin pistols loose at his hips.

"Why's all I want to know, Sheriff. He was such a good kid. Never hurt nobody I know of, not even a pup."

Pickler's voice was flexed by its adamant tone, authority straight and stiff in its delivery. "Course, you don't mean his brother Albie wasn't such a good kid either, do you, Jackie boy? Sayin' it twice don't make it nice."

"I didn't mean nothin' by it, Sheriff, just wonderin' who the hell'd want to kill poor old Nick Belotti. Makes no sense to me." The gray sombrero on his head shook with reaction, as though it was in sympathy with the youngster.

"Two sons off of one man is two too many no matter what way you look at it, Jackie boy, Sayin' it twice don't make it nice. Time'll let you know that when it comes around the way it allus does, out on the grass or up on the mountains." He wanted to say, "You gotta keep listenin' for the messages aimin' your way, Jackie boy," but managed to hold back on that delivery, thinking it over in a hurry as a waste of time and energy, the trade-offs almost visible to him.

The sheriff was figuring out how he was going to tell his best friend, Rico Belotti, that his second son was dead, and again by a sniper, a sure shot, from long range, and most likely coming all the way from old times. Old times and old crimes had connections one way or another.

Yet nothing in Belotti's past, and he figured he knew just about all there was to know, had or would have been told to him, all those card nights piled atop one another like stones in a wall a brickie set in place, like forever, a wall for protection, a barricade, yet as simple as keeping old pals out of the prairie sun.

There was something held back, some deed or daring completed long before the pair had met, leading to the murder of two sons, unthinkable to some men, especially men like Rico where the past is cast under a herd of hooves.

He kept thinking it over, trying to scrape up little pieces that had dropped out of hearing, the asides or mutterings at cards, winning a hand, losing a bigger hand, measuring things as they were.

His mind settled itself on the issue: It had to be money, cattle or women, he guessed, the only causes that came to mind ... and it made him think of seeing Maria Melody Belotti right away, one time in a cabin window making Rico's day for him, the new sun barely risen. That image never went away, hanging in his mind like a first kill, or the last whipping his father ever gave him, permanent as mountains looking downhill. "Such times can be sublime," he remembered. "A woman at giving is the best of living."

Possibly, there was a similar image hanging on for somebody else, another plain cowpoke, Maria being nothing but a plain knockout woman from first sight.

That memorable morning, Rico had come out of the cabin in the heart of the prairie, a world-beating smile on his face, a questioning look on his face when he saw his pal as red-faced as he had ever been ... which was like ... never, and looking as though an apology was at hand. Rico, aware of the situation, waved his hand, said, "Regular start of the day, Doyle. Happens all the time, now we got work to do."

He had mounted his stallion before his pal could move, or offer a statement.

Day, in a hurry of its own, had jumped on them good and proper.

Now, another day was on top of Doyle Pickler; he set about for his first duty of the new day.

Rico, at a window, saw him coming down the road, no hurry in his gait, a certain stiffness in his riding, the way he might ride alone in his own procession. He knew the awful feeling that he was getting a message before the message could be delivered.

He called Maria to his side, putting his arm about her waist. "Doyle's coming for a visit, Maria, an early one."

The quick stiffness in her body shook through him.

"Oh, God, Rico, he's riding like he did before, so slow, oh, so slow."

She shivered again, blessed herself, muttered, and clung to her husband.

The visit was short. The temporary sheriff saying, at length, "I'm stayin' 'til we get answers, Ma'am, Rico. I'll do the best I can to find out who and what and why," the sternness and promise carried in each word, as if his oath was mounted and saddled.

As he turned to go, he stopped, looked back at Rico, and said, "I know it all, Rico, that right?" The question loomed as though it ran through a courtroom, and came out on the other side of the open delay.

When Rico replied, "You got all of it, Doyle," he caught a quick look from Rico's wife that he'd have to dwell on, determine if it was a warning, a sharing, a condemnation of her husband, perhaps an all-in-one grimace, if it was a grimace to be understood at the moment of delivery.

"Women," he thought, "have a way about themselves. They're more informative than we dare think, often holding a fact or an idea closer to secrecy than we think, wondering when, where and why they can let it go, cause of causes, mystery of mysteries."

Doyle Pickler, for the next few days, kept thinking about that scene in Rico's kitchen, trying to wrap his mind around every word, movement, facial expression, and momentary silences that stayed with him. Often, and in turn, each one demanded explanation, further discussion, clarity.

Doubt about anything else coming from Rico made him more than nervous. The Belottis had lost two sons, but they had a daughter, Sofia Amanda, a beautiful girl almost in her twenties, married early as the custom, moved out with her husband, had a new baby, away from danger, or so it seemed.

From a distance, he promised himself, he'd keep watch and hoped for sudden or accidental revelation of causes behind unexplained murders. Chance or plain stupid luck was often a participant in the arrival or discovery of important clues and data. Of course, he never counted on it, wouldn't say a word of that nature to his deputy, but being alert to all matters, physical, emotional and at-all-possible, they lurked about in his attention span; he was not a dummy, he assured himself.

He was sitting at the bar a few days later with a couple of pals when a stranger entered the saloon, thin, somewhat inconspicuous, unarmed to the quick glance, no unexplainable bulges. The man slithered to the far end of the bar, his light, airy voice saying, "Beer, please."

31

The bartender poured the beer, and then spun about in place and sent a knowledgeable facial expression to the sheriff at the far end of the bar, who leaned forward over the bar, waiting to hear what was unsettling the barkeep.

"Sheriff," the barkeep whispered, "that new fellow down there is Slats Peabody. I seen him in court some years back, maybe ten, and he was sentenced to Kingston Jail for rustling and some associated deeds of the kind. I'm guessing he must have just got released, done his time, but can't figure what he's doing in here. He's a mean one in jail I heard, Even Jessie Wilks the stage driver heard talk about him. Fact is, he ain't goin' to any party an' got no family 'round here."

The sheriff strode down along the bar and addressed the new man in town. "Peabody," he said through the edge of his teeth like he was also trying to say something else, "I'm the sheriff here and I know you just got out of a cell in Kingston. I want to know who and what brings you here, how long you think you're gonna hang around lookin' for work or friends or old rustlin' pals who ain't here anyhow."

The sheriff was crowding Slats Peabody close to the bar, satisfied he was not armed, and said, "If I buy you another beer and you tell me who, what and why, I'll let you stay the night before you mount up and move on. That sound like a good deal to you?"

"Tell the barkeep to fill it to the top this time, Sheriff. I'm just lookin' for a friend I met in the hoosegow. Said he had something special up this way and to look him up if I ever got a chance. He was a quiet dude behind bars but I bet he's got somethin' special pullin' him all this way. Kept it all to himself, he did, but I saw it in his eyes, a kind of payback glow or a dream he can't forget, you know, the kind of stuff you go to sleep on and it sure wakes you up again first thin' o' the mornin' you ever been there in the first place."

Peabody plain stopped right there, as if he'd said too much to begin with.

Pickler held his hand up to the barkeep to hold up on the beer he had poured for Peabody, followed by a direct and hard eye on the ex-jailbird, saying, "The name, Peabody, the name of your pal or you go nowhere you like but somewhere you must be plain old sick and tired of."

He was still holding back the barkeep when Peabody, in the low voice of a secretive whisper, said, almost as an aside, but peacock-proud even breaking a sworn confidence, "Sawbuck Britten, the one and only, best break-in man in the west, ladies man, land-grabber, you name it and he's done it. There ain't no place he ain't been or no deed he ain't got done, for one kind of reason or another, and he's been my pal for a long spell, a magician, you ask me."

32

Peabody finished off his beer, and left without a further word, the saloon suddenly empty without him, and without the sheriff who left by the back door, bound for Rico Belotti's ranch, knowing he couldn't pass up the possibilities swimming in the back of his mind, right alongside Maria Melody Belotti's one-time grimace. There lingered hidden clues, hidden angers, hidden enmities, all life rolled into connected balls. And accident and fact have strange ways of getting locked up together, or "one good tern or one bad tern deserves another," as his bird-loving father once said to him, the joke and laughter loitering in his voice, a man with many talents, many intents.

Indeed, odd assessments were allowed to lighten Pickler's day. He'd remembered another one.

Maria Melody Belotti saw the sheriff coming down the trail to their home, the evening sun setting behind him, remembering what her husband had said on an earlier visit, how the sheriff sat his saddle, the message of death coming at them, now the messenger was coming again, all that was left was their daughter, miles away, a new baby at her breast.

Her heart sank; the Devil, she knew, often made amends in life, getting even for a bad time with similar payment, the messenger somehow attached to all of it. Was their old friend now employed by the Devil? She dared not think about her daughter ... but the thoughts pounded at her guilt, unintended, unwanted, part of her stolen in life and scratching to get back. She had not told her husband about the attack by a stranger, knowing in her heart she had been impregnated, Rico proud as ever thinking it was his baby. The stranger, as he left, advising her, "You've been introduced to the one and only Sawbuck Britten, scourge of the whole damned West, take my word for it."

He'd kissed her goodbye before he left her beside the trail. The gentle signs coming were signs she had known with her sons.

Was this sheriff coming on a repeat errand? Did he find any evidence about her sons? Had he found connections in their deaths? Was she going to be punished again? Should she try to blurt out the whole horrible truth before everything in life was turned upside-down?

She took hold of her husband's arm and said, "Doyle's coming again, like before. I know something's wrong."

He shook his head in the negative; there was not a clue or fact unseen. He was clean of blame of any kind. His sons' deaths were accidents. They had to be. Even if life stunk to the high heavens. and all the way up. He did not think about his daughter for one second.

Maria Melody Belotti spoke even as the sheriff entered her home: "Is it about Sofia Amanda? Please don't tell me it's about Sofia Amanda."

"No," smiled the sheriff, "I'd received some information and followed it up and staked out her home and found a man who said he was going to tell her that he had killed her brothers, but that's when he tried to draw on me, so I shot him dead on the spot. He never told me why. I guess it was just a lie."

Maria Melody Belotti asked, "Did he not say a word about why?"

"Not a word, Ma'am. Not a word. He took what he knew to the grave. Nothing shared is nothing bared. My father said that to me when I was a kid, all those years ago. I remember it every now and then. Can never tell you when."

In 1865, at the end of a long day in a long war, Corporal Thadeus "Ted" Walters was separated from the Army of the Union, with five years of service and a wound whose anger might hang in place. As a messenger between outfits of that conflict of interests, Corporal Walters was apt, on any day, to be in territory controlled by a Union force.

He saw many places and many faces, and was fired upon between message centers en route.

Comrades, and friends of a certainty, came out of his associations, and that included words of advice from some folks "who had been elsewhere and remembered."

One of them, a true horseman, and a volunteer from Day One of the war, said, "Ted, you gotta go west, get that sunshine square on your back and in your soul. I'll tell you this, on a pile this high of the Good Book, you'll never turn around and come back." He ended up adding, "I'm heading back to Montana myself so I could travel much of the way with you if you want company." His name was Larry Birch, a former lieutenant of arms and a most likable sort of fellow-in-arms.

Replying, Ted Walters let Birch in on his intentions of this "after-life," meaning the period right after the war and to where he was headed in it. "All well and good, Larry, but whenever I find a piece of heaven right here on terra firma, the smallest piece that comes my way, it'll be out of nowhere each time, I'm positive. But I'll know it on sight, or it'll grab me by the hand and pull me in, right on top of the glories abounding there. So I always stop to soak in that true light and I sure didn't find many in this war. It's a lock you'd get tired of me 'cause I never get tired of staying a while in any single piece of heaven that comes my way, fortune having a hand in the matter. And, for the sake of argument, it might be an eternity before you'd get all the way to Montana."

The two went their separate ways, and a few weeks later Ted Walters found a piece of heaven right under his feet, or his horse's hooves, in Pennsylvania in a village of Miami Indians who talked a strange language but made his restlessness fall right out of the saddle. One of the Miami braves, Crow's Flight by name, had been in the war and picked up a good bit of English, and served as an interpreter between the Miami tribal chief, Long-wood Walks, and Walters.

After several days at the site, Walters and Crow's Flight sat with the chief. Crow's Flight said, both languages in turn, "I have told the chief about your pieces of heaven and earth. He is in touch with our Great Chief of the Skies, and understands your own ideas of heaven and its god, and he says you may stay here as long as you like, though he feels that you must be seeking all the pieces so that you can put them together in one great heaven. 'That,' he says in judgment, 'is admirable.'"

Walters was amazed at the conversation and told Long-wood Walk, through Crow's Flight, that he had planned to be on his way the next morning.

The chief and Crow's Flight spoke quickly and Crow's Flight advised Walters, "There will be a dance tonight in your honor. Long-wood Walk will arrange all of it."

When the loveliest of all the tribe's maidens danced a special dance for Walters and offered her hand to him, he refused, knowing he'd not be able to leave her in the morning, she was so beautiful, one of the loveliest creatures he had ever seen, never mind her being offered up to him, a complete stranger at her threshold.

The chief understood the weight and expanse of Ted Walter's journey and let him go on his way. Two weeks later on that segment, Walters was caught up by the beauty of a valley in Indiana, so he stayed two weeks among the high hills, saying, "I know I'm in a piece of heaven here on this earth. There's no doubt in my mind, and my soul says it's so."

The mysterious rhythms were on course, in the air he breathed, in the rustle of leaves greener than any green he had known to date, and that included previously parts of heaven he had come upon ... or had been put in his way, for noble indeed was his journey.

He wandered about the area for those two weeks, finding peace and serenity at every turn, an almost silent music finding his ears in the solemn way silence has in its favor, every note coming to him through its own absolute journey from the Grand Master of all music.

But, the yearning moved about him, even as he remembered the beautiful Indian girl who had grasped his hand, his nightly dreams finding some others like her, even back before his military service where he lived just north of Boston.

Next, his travels took him into Iowa, to the little town of Scatterling, on the edge of a river that murmured for him first in a soft tone, then sang songs for him in a stretched-out tone. The river also shot sunlight back into the sky, that found him staring also at a most beautiful widow with a year old child. Her appeal to him was monumental, filling his dreams in a hurry at night so that they woke him up in a state of terror that he might not finish his journey. The dreams, and her beauty, made him forsake a love he might seek forever.

"Ted," she had said, "I do not understand why you can't stay with me. Did the war twist you onto that saddle of yours and make you a traveler for always, never to find your place of happiness here with me?" Her eyes set on him, the fire and sudden love in them lighting up her face, her full countenance, her total body at a near motionless rhythm as though it would hypnotize him on the spot.

She implored him to stay, a hand reaching, a touch of loveliness in its promise. "You can only go if I let you. Maisy and I need you." She was adamant about her needs. "There are things you should know about me, Ted. The hidden spirit lingering for companionship, for the truest of loves. Do you crush my heart so easily, though I can appreciate the journey you have carved out for yourself, a journey which must have its rises and falls along the way. You need to be careful."

The difficulties in assuming his travels bothered him, a sudden doubt about reality rising from the darkness lingering in his mind, only to be squashed in a hurry by an unknown power at its fatal work ... somewhere, somehow some place and someone was at this moment waiting for him. Destiny might be its name, or Fate, or Heaven in a circle of boundless calm, serenity, peace and beauty.

Thus, with a sheer beauty trying to keep him in one piece of heaven at its full promise, Nebraska and Wyoming and other wonder sights called him. Always, it seemed, a voice as distant as clouds mated with a disturbing golden moon called to him, the words, the messages, coming continually in dreams, days naps, sometimes in a sleep at riding as his horse gentled its way in a now-and-then mile at a time. At those moments, nothing of the surroundings summoned him, no wonder of a spirit called his name. At such times he did not despair, full of a belief that he was just passing through the "bare spots prior to Heaven's Gates," as he might have called them.

Then, the way true Fate works its wonders, he was in, of all places, Montana, right smack in the midst of splendid mountain ranges, like a whole passel of them in one sweeping view that nearly took his wanting heart on its own journey. He wondered where his old pal and comrade Larry Birch had ended up, what peak had drawn him back this way, what river he himself had crossed to get where he now stood, had Larry crossed, perhaps months before him... his breath too catching up in him. Good old Larry had never told him Montana would be like this, and his words came back in a slight echo climbing the mountain trails: "I'll tell you this, on a pile this high of the Good Book, you'll never turn around and come back."

Oh, how right Larry was, exuberance grinding away inside him, and him anxious to go down into one of these appealing valleys, one with a stream singing its way through the heart of Utopia, though he knew the mountain ledge he was standing on was in a range named for the local tribe, the Absaroka Indians, the mountain named Francis Peak rising to more than 13,000 feet.

Water glittered, it seemed, in a dozen directions, in arrows and spirals of rivers and saucers of lakes and ponds, the richness of heaven on the earth itself.

Then the other hunger hit him, sharp as a cutlass or even an old bayonet on his wartime musket, what he knew made the world itself go 'round, and it started moving him downhill on its own, his mind fuzzy with a girl he knew in Boston, the Miami tribe maiden dancer with her extended hand, the widow with a daughter in Scatterling, girls and ladies, women by unknown numbers from unknown places, angelic, spirited, and lonely as he was.

From a lower ledge, letting his mount rest for a spell, he saw a large log cabin sitting on a slight rise above the junction of a river as it joined a small lake that slowed the river's downward flow. A master of the trade must have built the cabin, and one with an artful and scenic eye. He was flabbergasted at the site; not a log or board was out of place in the whole design, not a rock residing on the surface without a reason, a few trees appointed for shade, and a young blonde girl sitting on an open porch with a large pan on her lap. A knife was working deliciousness loose from a harder core. Her hands were petal-like, smooth, tender, intent at work. The Miami girl came back. Another girl elsewhere and when they went way, he suddenly realized that they were going away for good.

He said goodbye in a silent voice, his mouth left open as if he had sent the word after friends gone forever.

He stopped to ask if he could water his horse. The girl beamed looking at him, her eyes bluer than the sky above, the smile so real, so authentic, that he felt the contained vibrations that came with it.

Truly, Corporal Thadeus Ted Walters knew Heaven was at hand, his travels as near completion as possible, only a positive introduction was needed by each party, and soon taken care of.

The older man stepping out of the cabin, said, "I saw you coming down the mountain path, our first visitor in several weeks. I am Oswald Cutterly. I am a widower. This is my daughter Amy. She cooks for me, takes care of me. She's a marvelous cook, a marvelous sewer of oddest things, a magician at others."

"My name is Thadeus 'Ted' Walters, late of the Union Army, and looking here on Earth for another piece of Heaven, and by God, I think I've found it."

"I believe you have, son, the whole lot of it." He pointed at his daughter and said, "Have you ever seen a smile more beautiful than that?"

"No, sir, I have not, and this surely is my final piece of Heaven for which I have long been looking for. Heaven is mine."

Nicky Consolo, from horseback, was studying the situation down below on a valley road, and was only three days from jail in Valley High where he'd been tried and found innocent of murder. The verdict, we all know, never moves as fast as news of the charge, and he was prepared for the differences ahead.

Perhaps his intersession here would hasten such a reaction, another form of aiding and abetting the way some wheels spin about in this world of hurried decisions, no matter who or what stands in the way of a common sense look at circumstances. A sheet hung on the line gets blown every which way, an old adage says.

From his turn on the mountain trail, he'd seen the stagecoach twisted to one side with one broken wheel, and the driver and his shotgun companion and four passengers, milling about the scene, not fully aware of the full predicament. He wasn't sure if other passengers were still in the coach, They were bound for Caldon Station, more than 20 miles away of rough terrain, and it was doubtful if they'd finish this leg before dark even if help was already on the way ... perhaps another passing rider gone ahead seeking help.

Not a nice pickle to be caught up in, he realized.

He'd also spotted a broken-down and abandoned coach, an hour earlier, a mile or so off the main trail, two wheels broken, but two still whole. No body remains were visible and he assumed the cause had happened sometime in a distant past and had been left in place to linger until final dust encompassed the incident, would bury it from knowledge of any sort, an incident not seen may not have happened.

One of those wheels, his mind settled on him, could be retrieved from that old site, he was sure, but he'd need help.

He decided he'd gamble despite the worries and headed downhill. About a half mile from the coach he saw a pink kerchief waving at him. It had to be a woman's kerchief.

His interest heightened, a difference in the making, and visible, a step up from the presentation of a dream, or an idle thought brought on by the rhythms in a saddle.

A young woman greeted him as he rode up, her face sparkling, a smile of relief and surprise warming him instantly. There's nothing like beauty in motion, he thought, first thinking of a horse at a dead run, then an arrow in flight, like an eagle zeroing in on a target, and a mountain lion, a wolf, or any meat eater, just before a leap, poised in the art of a hunt. These were natural actions and reactions to him, demanding scrutiny, possession to the depth of each image.

Keepers, he thought, the good keepers.

Surprise at the gallery of images she had freed for him, the others mostly standing about uselessly, except for the shotgun rider who had not yet dropped his rifle from immediate attention, but who had kept it level in his hands, as if his finger was on the trigger already.

Two figures, thus, from the group caught up in the middle of nowhere, demanded his attention, though he realized what he looked like to the members of this collection of folk, good or bad; a lone rider in the middle of a trail, coming from what-in-heaven, to where's-he-going-next, and alone at that.

Lone riders, many people of the roads, ways and byways of mountainous trails, wide open prairies, and all elsewheres, carried stigmas via initial judgments, guesswork, early impressions that somehow keep working in one's brain as if posted there by truth, fact, the physical proof of clear-sightedness.

But none so clear when in the midst of hurry.

Consolo decided he'd have to keep an eye on the shotgun rider, wondering what he had in mind, what he might even know about him, a lone cowboy just freed from jail, any and all trails available for travel.

"Hell!" he muttered to himself, "I'll be damned sure to keep my best eye on her, beauty of beauties." She was returning a smile, the study of a gaze fixed on him, an immodest interest in him at that, a lone cowboy on the trail, and just let out of jail. Some folks would begin their considerations on one plane quicker than others.

That, he decided, had to be kept at attention too.

He said to the driver, named Earl Hannaby, "I saw a wreck of a wagon back off the trail with at least one wheel I could salvage with some help, like one man and a pair of horses off this team. Looks like it's the best we can do right now." He looked around for support of his plan.

Hannaby said, "Good idea, son, but who are you? Whatcha doin' alone out here? Where ya headed?" He was speaking for all of them, of course, routine but necessary for stagecoach drivers, like the captain of a ship.

Consolo replied, "Nick Consolo's my name. I'm just looking for the next job, and it looks to me I found it. You got two lady passengers that can't help and three men who could, one of them being your shotgun. You tell me who and I'll get it goin'."

"Okay, son," the driver said in a quick study. "I'm not much with a rifle, so my shotgun has to stay here, for the ladies' sakes. You take that gent who's the bigger of the other two, and the first pair of horses off the team and hightail it to get that wheel. That's the best idea we have, Get it goin'."

Even as he spoke, his hand reached out and pushed the shotgun down from its level position in the hands of his front seat helper. That companion, by name Max Harding, was a thin, wiry gent with eyes old as Methuselah, an outfit of clothes never washed or cleaned since being donned, and a sharp looking, brand new black Stetson topping his head, just as if an older one most recently had been blown away in a storm or, even likely, shot clean off his head by a keen shooter. The man brought a history with him, carried it.

Consolo knew there was a story in front of him, just like he carried a story himself: each of them to come out in some telling moment, the way stories come out of the past around campfires, or sitting at a bar in a saloon, or between prisoners behind steel bars of a small town jail in small towns in the middle of everywhere in the West where folks had stopped to catch their breaths.

Loneliness loosens tongues for strange company at odd situations. It was a given for all men of the saddle.

Consolo and one passenger, a fairly rugged-looking man who announced his name as Breck Bjorstum, after spelling it out, said on the way from one accident site to another, "That shotgun gent told me you're an escaped bandit, maybe a murderer, but I think you're also the salvation for all of us. We could be killed out here in the darkness tonight. This is our best chance."

He was riding one of the wagon's lead pair of horses, Consolo, holding a rein on the second animal, gave a quick reply, "I was tried and found innocent. The charge was trumped up. It's done, as far as I'm concerned, done, finished. They now have the guilty party in the cell I was in."

Bjorstum, shaking his head, said, "Strange things happen wherever we go. Sometimes there's justice on the scene and sometimes it never shows its head. But take it from me, I'd keep my eye on that shotgun ride if I was you. I wouldn't trust him cutting up a pie in even pieces."

At the site of the wagon remains, the two men, somewhat at a comfort with each other, managed to wrestle one wheel free and mount it on one of the wagon horses. They were back at the crippled wagon before dark, Bjorstum advising Consolo once more, "Don't forget what I said about that sidewinder shotgun. He ain't to be trusted for a minute of your life. That's what it'll come done to, I can feel it." It was like he had reached out and patted Consolo on the back.

With Consolo and the driver doing much of the work, the spare wheel was mounted in place. All looked well and they were ready to proceed to Caldon Station, 20 miles down the trail.

Consolo caught the slight turn in Bjorstum's head and went to his side, Bjorstum saying, "Those two have been whispering, the driver and the sleazy shotgun, planning to jump you and tie you up before we get going. All they're talking about is the reward money. They're damned serious. I'd hightail it if I was you."

He looked down at Consolo's pistol sitting in his holster. "You sure it's loaded, Nick? Can I see it?"

It was the first time he had called Consolo by name, and it found a quick roost in Consolo's mind, but he had earlier unloaded the weapon, a serious and nervous twitch working on him, like a calm before a storm, his mind at work. Something was out of place in everything in the immediate surroundings. Luck good or bad was on hand, circumstances up for grabs, the fair and beautiful girl with the pink kerchief staying her distance, he thought, as if being leery of him.

Doubts had come into place from too much comfort, him remembering his father's words from the last day they had spoken, "When things look like it's going to be roses forever, it's time to know it ain't."

Bjorstum, in a rapid move, yelled at the same instance, "I got his gun, boys. He hasn't got a gun. Get that rope and tie him up, and I want my fair share of the reward. He told me some cock and bull story of being cleared and we all know he's running from the law. That's why he's all alone out here, a murderer on the loose, you can bet your last dollar on that. Said he ain't been in a town since he left Valley High and there's a couple of places off the trail he probably ducked away from just getting here."

He waved the pistol again, a man in charge. "We got him now, boys and girls." His eyes fell on the young beauty; her smile came back at him, wide open, a shift declared in her sympathies, her best wiles working overtime, chance and choice for her clearer than ever before.

Nick Consolo measured all of them, male and female, passengers and coachmen, the lot standing in front of him; Max Harding with a loaded rifle, Breck Bjorstum waving an empty pistol the way a deranged man might wave it, with no target in mind, but any moving thing being a possible target.

The supposed outlaw on the run moved inches at a time, getting nearer to the rifle with each move, Harding not at all worried by the threat seeing the pistol, in desperate moments, being aimed at the outlaw, from an angle and distance nearly impossible to miss.

He leaped, as Consolo leaped, the rifle leaving his hands, his finger almost caught on the trigger guard, the loaded rifle in the hands of the lone cowboy on the loose. He screamed at Bjorstum still holding the pistol, "Shoot him! For god's sake shoot him! He'll kill us all and leave us where we fall!"

Bjorstum, sudden control in his hands, a superior smile of vengeance and greed marking his face, squeezed the trigger ... on the empty pistol, squeezed it again and again, only to realize he was now, in

42

this moment of acclaim and reward, at the other end of a bullet, his heart about to burst, Consolo aiming the rifle directly at him. His quick look at the young lady, saying what his mind knew, what she now knew, what he really was, nothing more than a treacherous and greedy coward.

Nick Consolo set everything straight, how the finish of this leg of their journey was due, Harding's rifle unloaded and cast aside, his own pistol reloaded, mounted his horse once more, said to all of them, "I was cleared of that crime in Valley High. I did get released. I am on my own now."

As he rode away from the group still standing stiff in place, he swore he could almost feel in one hand, his gun hand, the cold steel bars of the Valley High jail cell.

The Congo Kid Comes Home
(or The Sailor Goes Horseback)

Raven Narbaught received the letter at Boston's Charlestown Navy Yard when his ship landed on the 8th day of December in 1879. He'd been a sailor attached to or on the USS Alliance, a screw gunboat, since it was launched four years earlier at Norfolk Navy Yard, and had not heard a word for close to two years from his parents or any of his siblings. Never desperate because there was no communication for so long, he was nevertheless overjoyed at seeing his parents' names and address on the envelope handed to him by a Navy clerk. He knew it was a special day, the sea calm as ever in the seclusion of the harbor, a slight wind cutting into the background of the city slowly climbing upward, sailors from half a dozen ships at least had touched home or somewhere nearer home in every situation, he believed. They were a jaunty lot and he had enjoyed much of his time on ship, but was looking for a change. The thought of so many sailors nearer home made him pursue the thought as he opened the envelope.

The note inside said, "Dear Raven, Butta-Ken, Jan-red and Desmont, We have moved from New York to Arizona Territory, at a small settlement called Bettaville and send this letter to the last known of all your addresses. Three youngest have moved with us and the rest of you have made your ways elsewhere in the land. Find each other if you can, and then us. We wait to hear word from all of you, that black is ever beautiful, that home is a good memory, that each of you is well, and that you all promise to come see us in our new home. We are now living a ranch life and connect with cattle and the need for good grass. Deep love from Momma and Poppa En. Summer 1879, newly arrived here."

The new family voyage across America to a western territory was measured by Narbaught in comparison to other family voyages. In the bardic story-telling fostered in the family by both parents, he saw on an imaginary globe the trips made by ancestors within Africa, from its coast and across the Atlantic Ocean in chains, their purchase into slavery on southern plantations, their quick road north in many cases after the Civil War, and the final move of some of them across America to a new and perhaps final place of peace and contentment. News of the move settled in him a sense of relief and resolve that he'd do his part to fulfill his mother's wishes and his father's demands, each inherent in the letter.

Handsome Raven Narbaught, one of three blacks on the USS Alliance, had been injured in a Mediterranean harbor accident when a rope broke and he had fallen overboard, crashing down on a loading dock as supplies were being brought aboard. He was treated in a hospital and then on board ship on the long trip stateside, where he was discharged from naval service at Charlestown Navy Yard on the same day that his parents' letter finally caught up to him.

His injuries pretty well healed after some rest, he set out for Arizona Territory, his travel conducted in any available manner ... wagon, train, and horseback as he was performing a series of duties in temporary employment heading the same way. Naval training had drawn him to the exposure and use of all kinds of small arms, and his acumen brought him comfort and a degree of satisfaction in their employ. He was an expert shot, had a steady hand, and a degree of confidence that earned him decent and dangerous assignments on the way west ... patrol and guard duty, scouting to a limited degree (reminding him of spar watches when looking for icebergs in the northern reaches of the Atlantic), shotgun riding on stagecoach runs, and most generally as a regular cowpoke on cattle drives to railheads for delivery to markets east of the Mississippi River.

It was, plumb on, what his father had said in life's beginning lessons, "Learn while you earn."

Not sure of his natural talents at horse or gun, he improved both actions with dogged study, practice and determination. Without doubt, he became a stick-out rider and manager of all the horses he rode and the weapons he brought to hand. His horsemanship improved every time he saddled up and set out for a day's work ... and gunnery skills came with practice. Early he knew that he and his horse were one, fully bent on dependence. Soon came a kind of innocent wizardry with a revolver, that too due to practice.

Any degree of efficiency with handling firearms made life a bit easier and more promising than a bold and too innocent approach to western lands no matter if the lands had been incorporated into the Union as a state or remained as a territory. Laws were enacted in both places, and made life run fast for some folks beyond the great river, as it often found itself being directed by men who had little respect for it, who took what they could from where they could and from whom they could. Fast horses and quick and accurate weapons made life better, and longer in many cases.

For a black man, horse and gun had to be mastered.

Best be armed was more than a slogan; and it was, at the same time, a caution for former Navy sailors with black skin. Men like Narbaught were looked upon in different guises ... with fear, guilt, and a real sense of shame by a small per cent of westerners. If a man could ride, rope, shoot, tend the cows and remuda, watch the backside of a herd as well as the front, they fit the atmosphere about them.

So the black sailor turned cowboy worked his way into the new career, on a horse with a side arm in his holster and a rifle banked into a saddle sheath. He was not loath to use a weapon when it was needed, as against robbers, rustlers, brigands of any ilk, renegade Indians, war-time holdovers from different loyalties ... Union, Confederate, Mexican, you name a cause and he met up with its strange and beleaguered elements long before he got to the Arizona territories. Narbaught treasured these experiences, humorously thinking how they might stand out on his employment resume, provided he was still standing when it counted: sailor, wagon soldier and scout, shooter.

One other cause was that of gunplay, for self-defense or job requirements, each element hardened by the deep shade and color of his skin. That he was a handsome son of a gun also added to enmity, racism, and plain jealousy whenever anyone looked his way in mixed company.

All of it, from his perspective, came to light in a small settlement in Iowa where his blackness was treated with quick disdain before his horse was stabled for fixing. He made up his mind to steer clear of problems in the saloons where he was sure to be berated, challenged, drawn to gunplay, but thirst created other moves, like drinking at the back end of a livery when his horse was eventually being shoed, checked, and leather-repaired. It was another black man who accused him of ducking the issue of who he was by not getting his whiskey in the saloon just down the street.

"You ain't strong enough to face yoreself, heh? Where you been since the Great War got loose on us? Lost? Hidin' out?" The speaker was a light skinned black big as the side of a barn, dressed in black, wearing guns with barrels almost as long as his arms. "My name's Lucifer Hoovery, not black as sin, not black as Hades with the lights and the fires dead, but black and ready to go get a good stiff drink right down the street and anythin' that comes in tow with it. You comin' with me, or hidin' out here?"

The man stood out solid as a promontory in its rocky place, stone-hard, pinnacle tall, smoky black from a hot fire, and the light in his eyes saying what one found in his words, in the chisel-sharp tone of his voice, in the derring-do mustered by his singular presence. He was ready for lions, pumas, mountain cats looking for fresh meat, the meanest of taunters, those big mouths and loud mouths and supposed quick-shots who always shot off their mouths first at intention giveaways.

"Aye, aye, Captain," Narbaught said, accompanying his words with the snappiest of salutes. He tapped the sides of his holsters and said, "By the way, I am not empty handed."

"Damned glad of that, brother," Hoovery said. "We might be lookin' up a mountain in there."

Of course, there was a stir, then a silence of questioning, then a shuffling of feet, dispositions, and attitudes as the pair of black men walked into the Red Tail Saloon. The room was almost full, with several men standing at the bar, a few hands of poker on display at a few tables, a long mirror behind the bar almost as wide as two oxen in a yoke, atop which was a painting of a woman in thin bed clothes. Two bullet holes stared back from her breasts at any viewer. Two brass spittoons were prominent at the base of the bar and one of them also wore a bullet hole. The reasons for the bullet holes might prove obvious to a stranger; the room seemed to curry noise, boasting, challenges to gun or color or loyalties in any mix.

It didn't take long for the loudest loudmouth to get going.

He was a tough looking, wide-shouldered man, his Stetson tipped back on his head saying he was comfortable in the crowd, and a light mustache and a thin beard that said he hadn't shaved in a week or more. On probably all occasions he was the voice and the spirit, to some degree, of the lot of them. Wilhelm "Kick" Ruefacht had been a wrestler, a notorious one, back east somewhere, as he would tell it, offering many times to demonstrate his deadly kick to anybody who didn't believe his words. It would be a rare man who stood up and said so. And at this moment Ruefacht didn't knew he had another non-believer in front of him, talking like there was nothing around that'd disturb him much.

Ruefacht's body shook a little, a shifting of feet presented his full front to the two newcomers, and a half smile and half sneer curved his mouth before belligerent words came out of it.

"Wal, now, lookee what we got here." He was holding his arms outspread as if he was praying or waiting for some treasure to fall into them from on high. "Not from any ranch, these gents, but right off'n a cotton patch someplace down the line. And them thinkin' they's gonna drink with us." The last words were guttural, deep as a hole dug for burial. His eyes fell directly on Freddie Sketchum the bartender, saying the tap was closed for the moment, or else would happen.

Hoovery, in a steady voice that rolled the whole south into it as he spoke to the bartender, "Ah don't have a smitten if this place belongs to you, mister, but if my pal and me don't get us our couple a drinks thin's'll get awful messy 'round here. Now you contend with me and my friend, git us our two drinks an' we'll leave this fellow alone and yore place in the same peace where it is right now. Otherwise, the mess comes quicker'n you can think an' I believe my new pal is quicker'n me."

At which point he touched Narbaught on the shoulder. "I just met this fellow the very mornin' of the day an' somethin' 'bout him says he knows more'n all of us. He's been 'round the world in Navy ships." He shook his head in wonderment when he said that, smiled, and patted Narbaught on the shoulder again. "Ya'll know what they say 'bout sailors. What all'em ladies say, too."

47

He was as relaxed, as cordial as any man could be, whether he was lying or not. Most of the men in the saloon, including Freddie the bartender, were aware of him stretching things, but Ruefacht was oblivious of it, though many could see his hands slyly setting up for a quick draw of his side arm, and it appeared as if he had stopped his breathing for the fast action to follow.

Standing there, apparently useless, being protected by a stranger from another stranger, Narbaught recalled all his days learning the art of the holstered pistol quick draw. He too didn't appear to breathe when he stood there, his pistol suddenly in his hand, a steady hand, a hand that had not been seen to move, a smile on his face, as he said, "Mister, all we came in here was for a few drinks, not a lot of noise from a blowhard that wouldn't last the night aboard my ship if he kept talking like you do and if he couldn't swim in the first place. There is one chance for you to sum up your chances and take them elsewhere, because I advise you there will not be a second chance to apply them here."

He returned his pistol to its holster and stood there facing Ruefacht.

The silence consumed the air in the room until one voice in a far corner said, "Wal I'll be. Thet there is the fastest gun pull I ever did see, because I don't think none of us seen a gun move like that before, which makes me tell myself not to go on waggin' 'bout an'thin' else here lessen it's 'bout feedin' the hungry or pourin' for the thirsty, as the Good Lord says."

The speaker was gray with beard, bent with experience, and obviously marked by respect in the room.

He turned to the bartender and said, "Freddie, if'n you don't pour them two boys their drinks, I'll buy 'em and give 'em myself."

There issued a few "harrumphs" from the crowd in the saloon, but mostly arose a respectful silence as many of them wondered if they actually had seen Narbaught draw his gun. and nothing derisive was tossed off by an unknown voice … nor any support for the dumbfounded Ruefacht, still immobile in front of the bar, not having drawn his side arm and apparently not about to do so, showing awful good sense in refraining.

Between the livery and the Red Tail Saloon the bond between Narbaught and Hoovery had been cemented in place, ready for anything. A kinship had developed that might get both of them to Bettaville in the Arizona Territory to see Narbaught's family.

There were a few more incidents like this one on the way, close calls at taunting, racial slurs, but guns not drawn. And so came the new friends into Bettaville in the Arizona Territory on a June day in 1880.

Their first stop was for a drink in an unnamed saloon without doors. Bettaville seemed warm, honest and quiet, until they walked into the saloon where one man stood quickly, announcing that no coloreds were to be served in the place where he drank, "And I'm with some of my boys," he carefully added, nodding around the room.

To which Narbaught replied, "And I'm not alone either. I brought my guns, my pal Hoovery here, best shot I've met this side of the U.S. Navy, and we're not lost if you think that. We are not waywards or saddle bums, but we are going to visit my parents' ranch near here and I will repeat that such a visit will in no way be deterred by anybody here or elsewhere, as it has been a long time since I have seen them." He slapped his holster with a sudden move, and the slap sounded like half a gunshot.

The sound alone forced a silence in the room and all bodies remained stationary, as if frozen in place, including the lonely loudmouth standing like a tree in the desert, all by his self.

A man standing at the end of the bar said, "Is Fen-red Narbaught your father? Owns the old Grisby spread northwest of town. I was out that way last week. Him and your ma look well, and are as cordial as all get out. They was hopin' for some visits from you and some other kin."

He advanced down the bar, extended his hand, and said, "I'm Earl Sanford, a neighbor of theirs. If you're like your father, you're okay with me, son. And your pal, too. I only got one piece of advice for you both … you better get ready for work. It all ain't no plain social call out there."

The saloon crowd was softened by the words, and the bigmouth walked out by himself, and "his boys" slipped into anonymity within the saloon.

"What will they call it in the old language?" Sanford asked.

"*A kuwakaribisha nyumbani chama kwa ajili ya mwana*," Narbaught replied in Swahili. "It means a welcome home party for a son. If there's more than me, it'll be something else."

"Well, when I was there last week, an invited guest, your mother sang some chants in her language and I have never heard anything like it in my life. Pure enchantment it was, and I swear something was in her eyes like she knew you were coming home. Do they know you're coming? You send a letter?"

"Surprise is best for her. It's the way I'd like it, too," Narbaught said. "Her smile is extra special. My father rarely smiles."

"I noticed that," Sanford responded. "And I'd keep my eye on that gent that just left. He don't let things set too easy for others unless he gets his way on them."

"I'll remember that, Mr. Sanford. I surely will, especially the next time I see him."

It made Sanford smile.

As Narbaught and Hoovery rode over the last rise in the road to the Narbaught spread, they saw the smoke rising and heard random gunshots.

They spurred their horses and saw three horsemen firing at the small ranch house with a fire burning in one of two barns on the property. Return gunfire was coming from the ranch house.

"It's that blowhard from the saloon," Hoovery said, as he pointed out one of the riders, and Narbaught and he both started firing at him as they rode hard onto the scene. The attackers, surprised at shots from a different direction, broke for the road heading north, trying to escape the newcomers. Their shots cropped around the three men in flight, and from the house came a victorious yell in the old language, Narbaught's father, running out the door and waving his hands, yelled out, "*Sisi alijua wewe d kuja, kunguru. Kuwafukuza mbwa na makali ya Jahannamu na kushinikiza wasitoke Na kisha kuleta rafiki yako kwa ajili ya chakula cha jioni.*" He slapped his hands down on his thighs in more celebration and waved again and again, a revolver in one hand, his voice rising all the time.

The younger Narbaught thought his father was going to start dancing.

"Let me in on that," Hoovery laughed, as he let go another shot, saw dust lift up right behind one fleeing rider. "We sure got 'em on the run."

Raven Narbaught answered, "He said, 'We knew you'd come, Raven. Chase them dogs to the edge of Hell and push them in. And then bring your friend for dinner.'"

"I'm all for that," Hoovery said, and the new pair of pals rode hard after the attackers who disappeared in a series of rugged rocky formations and small canyons a mile down the road.

A high celebration duly took place at the Narbaught's new home, with an additional surprise, for they had received a letter from Butta-Ken who promised he'd be there in a month's time.

This was balanced a few days later by a visit from Earl Sanford. "The sheriff's comin' out this way today or tomorrow. They found one of Kick Ruefacht's pals shot in the back and dead in one of them canyons over yonder. Name of Liam Ford. Ruefacht said they was playin' around out near here and you fellows chased them off with gunfire, and now one of 'em's dead, Ford like I said. Sheriff'll be askin' some questions. I'd be ready for anythin' if I was you folks. He might be favorin' Kick in this, 'cause he's got a gun wound too, along his arm." He drew his hand across the back of his shoulder and down one arm. "It sure don't look good."

In the midst of cleaning up the section of a barn that had caught fire, with the Narbaughts and Hoovery pushing hard at the task, the sheriff came with a deputy.

"I've got to talk to you folks. Kick Ruefacht says you were shooting at him when they was horsing around. One of his boys, Liam Ford, must have got hit 'cause he fell off his saddle out there somewhere. They brought him in. I got his story now I need yours."

The elder Narbaught said, "That gent and two of his pals were shooting up our house, almost killed my wife, started a fire in one of my barns, left a mess of bullets in the walls of the house, which I'll show you shortly, and they were driven off by my son and his pal who showed up in a surprise visit. Chased them until they disappeared in those canyons down yonder, knowing the territory better than any of us did."

"That ain't nothin' like he said," replied the sheriff.

"So where does that leave you, Sheriff?" Hoovery said. "I think he was so mad and is so mean and ornery that he let his own man die with that wound, like a real coward would."

"That don't seem likely," the sheriff answered.

"Well, Sheriff, we stood him down in the saloon, me and Raven here, and he backed off like a coward and you think we had to shoot him in the back. Shoot a coward in the back? That's one part that don't seem likely to me, bein' an old lawman myself back there in Kane County, Illinois. It looks like you got to talk to his other pal who was here. You talk to him yet?"

"No, I haven't. Ain't seen him around yet since Kick made the claim against you folks." Then, with a puzzled look on his face saying he wasn't so puzzled about something on his mind, the sheriff asked Hoovery, "When was you there, in Kane County?"

"Oh, when Sheriff Sammy Beard got some trouble on his hands, died in the middle of it and the coroner Georgie Taffe took over the job, then kilt hisself, probably over nothin'. But it was a good place to steer clear of and I had the chance so I git out here and was lucky to meet Raven and his folks, but it's a strange way to meet someone by havin' to protect them from raiders or killers."

"Ain't nobody charged with anythin' yet, even me comin' out here to hear you folks and what you had to say on the matter."

"Oh, you got all we got, Sheriff," Hoovery said. "An arrest can't be far off," and he winked as he looked at Raven Narbaught.

Raven stepped in before too much was said, or asked, his mind clicking clear as a new gun mount. "What's the name of Ruefacht's other pal, Sheriff?" He was flashing a smile full of teeth white as sails out on the water of a lake.

"Jeb Wilson, calls himself." The sheriff shifted uncomfortably, as if bothered by a new image. When he wiped his brow with a great red kerchief that had been knotted on his belt, and then his deputy did the same maneuver, all the Narbaughts knew the sheriff was worried about something.

"I have a suggestion, Sheriff," Raven Narbaught interjected quickly. "My friend and I will go find this Jeb Wilson and bring him right down to your office and you can question him, not us. That fair? No funny stuff. Just plain citizens out for the good of the old folks." He pointed to his parents. "I know they'd appreciate your assistance in this matter, same as other folks like Mr. Sanford would, another stand-up citizen like yourself. That good with you, all on the up and up?"

The sheriff understood he could not say much against that plan, so he didn't. Perhaps Kick Ruefacht would stand alone one time in this life. He nodded his assent and he and his deputy rode off.

It did not take Raven Narbaught and Lucifer Hoovery very long to find Jeb Wilson. Too many people in and around Bettaville had seen the elements that surrounded Kick Ruefacht and were pleased to tell the pair what they knew about them, and point the way to places they knew where they often spent secret time away from the town … for one reason or another.

One of the places was an old line camp not more than a dozen miles away, at the end of an up-hill slope of green grass and built against a cliff wall where the first of the mountains emerged. A pile of logs sat at one end of the camp, the log ends showing white newness in the stack. An ax leaned against the pile like a last breath had left it there. No smoke emitted from the thin chimney. Two horses were tied off at the side of the cabin under a lean-to when Narbaught and Hoovery first sighted the building. Neither horse was Ruefacht's big gray with one white stocking on a foreleg. The only movement, other than a swish of a horse's tail, was a gray-white jackrabbit bobbing on a grassy spread.

Hoovery said, "That paint belongs to one of the shooters at your Pa's place. I bet it's Jeb Wilson's horse. He got some kind of a surprise comin' his way now." He had a look on his face that Narbaught had seen before, even as Hoovery finished saying, "We do it careful or noisy? They don't expect company way out here this early in the day."

He talked like the old law hand he used to be in Kane County, and Narbaught let him make the plans of taking a prisoner.

In 15 minutes time they were at the side of the small shelter where the two horses were tied off. Hoovery, as planned, untied one of them and slapped him on the rump, which made the horse gallop off noisily.

Commotion started in the cabin. "One of the horses is loose," yelled one inhabitant, and a second voice said, "That's your horse, Jeb. Get my horse and go get him. I'll check around for what made him break away."

The last talker came to the lean-to, and walked right into the guns of Narbaught and Hoovery. He raised his hands slowly and said, "I ain't done nothin'. Better talk to Jeb. He's got a lot to say. Been talkin' all night. I ain't even slept over it. He's scared to death of Kick Ruefacht. Thinks he's gonna kill him if he finds him. He was goin' to light out of here today, go north somewhere. Real scared."

Narbaught said, "Be careful and call him back here. Don't scare him. We don't want to hurt anybody."

He shook his gun under the man's face. "You with me on this? Real careful like?"

"Yup," the man said, and yelled out, "Better come see this, Jeb, how he got loose. You won't believe it."

Jeb Wilson also walked into the drawn guns of the two black men holding his pal at tight quarters. An amazed look crossed his face, one that also showed some sign of relief had come upon him.

"Well, Jeb," Narbaught said, "You feel better that we came for you rather than your pal, Ruefacht?"

"He ain't my pal. He shot Liam right in the back of the head to blame you folks, just like it was nothin' at all and told me to keep my damned mouth shut or I'd get the same."

Hoovery said, "Will you tell the sheriff that and swear to it in front of a judge?"

"I sure will if you got Kick all locked up in the jail."

"Oh, don't worry none about that," Hoovery said. "We got that all covered too. The sheriff just doesn't know 'bout it yet."

For the time being at least, the sailor was home from the sea and his pal was far away from Kane County in Illinois, which for some reason mattered a lot to him and some folks in Kane County.

In Bristol Hills, Oregon and Newville Point in Iowa, in early 1847, troubles leaped about the two townships related in more ways than one. Oregon, for example, was still a Territory, while Iowa had attained statehood a year earlier. But status didn't play favorites in any quarter in those days where thugs, robbers, killers and kidnappers often were the order of the day, to use a phrase for the misbegotten, abused, broken in pocketbook and spirit, subject to doctoring if they were lucky.

Times were risky, and many men thought salvation was carried in the holsters on their hips, or, for long range corrections, the rifles in their saddle scabbards.

There were choices at base level.

The facts are that statehood celebrations in Oregon didn't come until 1859, when part of the Oregon Territory became a state of the union, as Texas had in 1845 (from the Republic of Texas) and not-too-distant Iowa had in 1846, from part of the Iowa Territory. Lawful deeds in states of the union were legal, easy enough said, whereas unlawful deeds brought out the badges in official manners, and in a hurry in a few small towns as new states felt the lawlessness. It came brooding from odd depths of feelings, from anger and spite, from avarice that old games and easy money were somehow considered illegal, that badges on the chest had to have behind them a heavy constitution, a good hand, and courage galore to wear it, a loud proclamation to say the least. And, easy to understand, the right to carry weapons.

Changes were being organized ... on both sides of laws protecting the populace in general, the cattle ranch owners, miners, sheep men, shop owners, saloon keepers, etc., the run of the mill touch at work. It might have meant "Work or be damned" for most of the population, but not those richly endowed or those wanting the same via different routes and methods. The *yet* that applies here is both upper and lower echelons were targets of choice for as many hungers as there are choices within the souls of men and women.

The mayors of two towns, days apart in travel, but closely knit by family bloodlines, had long-range discussions via newer telegraph systems that had leaped across the country, east to west, about helping each other as each locale had become, seemingly, the center of ravage, savage and, of a certainty, retribution, often as severe as the subject crime.

Mayor Cal Clifton of Newville Point in Iowa said to his cousin, Harry Comerford in Bristol Hills, Oregon, "How's it going for you, Cal, way out there almost on top of the Pacific Ocean? You got a good sheriff to handle the riff-raff for now? Carson Jobb, is it? You mentioned his name before. He have a good gun hand or is he the regular tough guy on a tough job, not likely to kill a man if he can help it, no matter what the critter's done? Not like my man, a true gunsmith, with a poetic handle to boot. Strong Long's his name."

One mayor could almost hear the chuckle in the other mayor's voice.

There was, however it may have developed, unspoken intent at two levels in Clifton's message: he wanted to help his cousin, meaning aid to a family member, and get rid of a pesky fast gun who happened to wear a badge. At least, seek a little rest from the constant parade of criminal deaths; it could get sickening, jingles being written and sung openly, that he didn't want to hear for a while, get a break, give good old Harry a shove in sheriff's operations, *The Starry Era* as it was being called in many quarters of Newville Point:

> *What don't belong is a man named Strong.*
> *Why's a Star hanging by the bar?*
> *Want to get sick? Stick close to Star's too-damned slick.*
> *Watch a gun get good and done. It sure ain't a ton o' fun.*

Comerford, tired of the dilly-dally and the musical puns, was all for the swap of badge wearers, so it was done: mutual aid, he opined, was the coming thing in law enforcement.

Indeed it was, and in a hurry.

Iowa's fast-gun sheriff was wearing an Oregon badge, Star of Stars, when he strolled into the Elbow's Rest Saloon in Bristol Hills for the very first time, less than an hour after arrival and badge-pinning. Two steps into the saloon, the word on him well ahead of his new territory of responsibility, he was greeted by a crackling, high-pitched voice at a near table, saying snidely, "Oh, my, here comes the new sheriff, a fast gun as they say back home wherever the hell he come from."

The speaker stood as though he was still caught between his chair and the table. He wore a black sombrero tipped back on his head, a raggedy and off-colored shirt that fit him as though it belonged to a heavyweight, and dark denim pants worn to a frazzle and tucked into his riding boots.

Long studied the man, marked him as blowhard, big mouth, show-off for table companions who might well have been talking about the new sheriff before he even stood before them. Even might have dug up the challenge to hurl at the sheriff, to cast greetings in a way.

Strong Long, in his usual and unperturbed voice, said, "Well, *Mouthy*, if you have guts enough to back up your mouth, and are faster than a slow donkey at his deplorable work, and have any guts at all in your skinny gut, make a play."

The words came as steel, and as cold, and yet bounced like a drum in the otherwise silent room, all eyes having moved from the new sheriff to the mouthy customer, slowly trying to move away from the table, a man who could be on his way to jail ... or death, as the word had been carried to them all the way from Newville Point in Iowa.

Long, we must know now as well as ever, had seen all the false moves, and had seen this move recently, at least several times, a fake trip when rising from a chair or from a crouch or from kneeling, trying to throw a target off-stride, catch him unawares, get the pistol free of his own holster before the lawman could get to his pistol.

That was not about to happen. Not right then. Not in front of the crowd at the Elbow's Rest Saloon in Bristol Hills, Oregon. Not on a highly-touted and proven gunner ... with a Star on his chest.

The mouthy man died from a bullet right through his heart, and fell with a loud thud onto the floor, the slug ending up in the wall behind the bar, scaring hell out of the barkeep who once had swung a rifle onto a mad drunk ready to shoot up the place.

This time was different.

Long, putting a new bullet into his pistol chamber, said to the dead man's table mates, "You gents take your pal outside and do what you have to do with him in this part of Oregon."

He went to the bar, said to the shaky barkeep, "Sorry for the mess, but it was real agitatin'. And might as well pour a drink for me, of the good stuff, mind you."

Back in Iowa, in Newville Point, the Iowa star was pinned on Carson Jobb by Mayor Cal Clifton in a quiet ceremony, the mayor saying, "I expect to have a really quiet time around here, Mr. Jobb. Please see to it with your usual smooth tactics. I am impressed with your credentials. At that moment his secretary walked in and said, "Just got a telegraph from your cousin. Long just killed a man out there, like he's holding onto his old way of doing business. The first man, he says, who stepped up to face him."

Three days later, two more deaths in Bristol Hills, Cal Clifton breathing easier by each report, came another telegraph report all the way from Oregon: "Sheriff Long killed by assassins' bullets, two of them from different directions. I need Cobb back here pronto."

The mayor called in his new sheriff. "I got to send you back, Sheriff Cobb. Strong Long's been killed and the mayor needs you back in Bristol Hills. Which of our two deputies, in your opinion, should I appoint as sheriff, now that you're leaving us?"

"The young one, Pearson," Cobb replied immediately, without any compunction.

"You sure about that?"

"Yes, sir, I am."

"Okay, I'll do it. You have a good trip."

Cobb, at the door on his way out, said, "He's a better shot than Long was, and quicker, if you was to ask me that." His parting smile was less than serious.

He closed the door on the man behind him, closed it on the mayor, on the office, on Newville Point itself.

Back in Bristol Hills, Cobb sat with the mayor, who advised him of details of Strong's death.

"No other details?' Cobb said. "No sudden enemies saying odd stuff, getting even stuff? No loud curses? No threats? No witnesses, I'd gather? The town not so quiet since I left." Both men totally aware that the current attempt at mutual aid had not worked as intended.

"Not a whisper, I swear," replied the mayor, who added another observation, "I have a few good listeners out there who'll always report back even the smallest rumor if they think it'll interest me. Not a word yet from any of them, like they're afraid to speak up, afraid of getting tangled in a new affair."

"Do one favor for me, Mayor, find out from your sources who else was at the poker table when Strong went into the saloon that first night and had to shoot that man."

"Oh, I know who they are." He scribbled names on a small pad of paper. "There were five others. Their names are here on this list. Strong himself told me who they were. Do you think they're suspects?"

"Not an idea with me, but I'll think about it now." He nodded at the mayor with a facial expression the mayor might spend hours trying to figure out ... and get no place further than he was at this moment.

Cobb, his old star in its old place, thus began his observation of the five poker players, from any and every angle, from his office window, from the window in his room above Garvey's General Store, from horseback behind bushes, rocks, promontories, cave mouths, fallen logs or limbs or rotted tree trunks, from every conceivable spot where he could remain out of sight while keeping note of one subject at a time, or when two or more of them met away from the saloon.

In less than a month back on the job, Cobb detected two of the men shared more time together than with any of the other poker players, which was some days none at all with the others. One man was Jim Spooner, tall, thin, graceful in some manner, and who looked like a tested cowboy when in the saddle. The other one was Carl Laskey, rugged, a bit bow-legged, thick across the shoulders, slower in some movements than Spooner showed, appeared stolid and firm in all his movements whether in the saddle or not. He decided Spooner, from his acute observations, was the weaker of the two men, and thought he'd break loose first with some kind of inside information about Long's death.

Cobb was willing to bet on it.

From a list of notes he had started about the two men, he knew where he would find Spooner on a couple of days of the week ... visiting the widow Cassidy at her home outside of town. On Cobb's first attempt to talk to Spooner alone, he surprised the Cassidy visitor before he reached her porch, stopping him in his tracks from behind a huge rock where he had studied him before.

"Hold it right there, Spooner," he said, his pistol leveled at the surprised rider. "We got some serious talking to do about murder of a sheriff and come the hanging of two killers, all in one breath. Your pal Laskey said you brought up the idea of the two of you, getting Sheriff Strong in double rifle sights where it'd be difficult to pin his death on one man, and getting clean away from it. How's that strike you? Your best pal shooting his mouth off like that, leaving you alone on my promise to take it easy on him. You know how stupid he is, don't you?"

"I don't believe you," Spooner retorted. "He wouldn't do that to me, not when he thought it up himself, even hid both rifles so they'll never be found."

"Where'd he hide them?"

"He's not that stupid."

Cobb's smile came wide once more. "He got me here, didn't he?"

He waited for Spooner to just about fall off his saddle when Aggie Cassidy yelled out a loud "Hello" from her porch.

On the way back to town, one prisoner in tow, he knew the word would spread like a fed fire, sort of a mutual help system at work: tracking down a runaway like Carl Laskey would be a cinch; he felt for the bunch of notes in his shirt pocket, loosed a smile for nobody in particular.

In the year 1736 they had gone through Powhatan country and Cherokee country on their way west and were still heading south to escape winter trails, well after the "twin births" of sons came about at the beginning of the year and then at the other end of the same year, establishing their birthdays to be celebrated at the mid-point of succeeding years on the long, long trail west.

Parents, it has long been practiced, must heed the celebration of children's birthdays, especially for two boys born in the same year.

Then through Chickasaw country they had gone after varied New England native settlements and Comanche country, and our hero, Welcome Walcott, once of the North of Scotland and his wife *MariaMary* or *Two Ms* or *Double M* or *MaryMaria* or plain *Mary you,* and it well could have been *pi, pigh, pie*, for all of it. But she knew the differences the names made (the tone of voice, the tip of his head like a directional, the lights almost flashing in his blue eyes right out of the Scottish highlands), for he was her man, her with the two boys at her skirts, two look-a-likes for sure, twins many thought in whatever train they joined in Indian country of one tribe or another, on their way west for a dream home sitting in her mind that only Welcome, her man for all of life, could create.

Heading west in those days, as it was with the *Welcomes here we come*, meant they had to wagon-up with folksy trains en route, the more the merrier, the safer each passenger was, especially those bearing arms, as did Walcott Welcome. He carried a homeland Brown Bess Musket Rifle, an 0.75 caliber flintlock, a British land forces standard long gun since the year of 1722 or thereabouts, often changing odds, fortunes, and many of the ruling orders wherever it was employed.

In Chickasaw country came the first questions about the boys, then five years old and the image of each other, twins for sure, they had to be, like they were split from the same pod in the very beginning, and who were named by their father as Willard and William, Bill I and Bill II, still locked together whether by deep intent and mere accident. Walcott said, "Let it all be," as if that was the end of the duplicity. But MaryMaria, or Two Ms, with every opportunity, had a few words of explanations when the boys were decided by others to be twins.

"Conception," she said, "in the same year of two sons is the good Lords' doing and my welcomes to Welcome, as we must surely call it what it is. I am all the happier about it, and someday," a faraway look coming into her eyes, "when these boys are men and must walk away from us, we'll stand at the doorway of our home full of sadness and completeness."

She was a dreamer and she was lying, of course, which will be explained down the line, in this story of Welcome Walcott and his family.

Some women listening to MariaMary, not knowing a good second of truth in the matter, nodded their heads and some men shook their shoulders as if she was a simple woman with a dream too big to handle.

Deep in Comanche country, the wagon train beset by the second fierce raid in a week, Welcome Walcott, with his Brown Bess knocked the most decorated and highly-colored Indian right off his horse with a single and pronounced shot, scattering all remaining raiders from sight after they had retrieved the body of their chief, as assumed by Walcott before he had said, "That pretty one out front is mine."

MariaMary had loaded his weapon for him, even as she huddled the two youngsters behind a barrel of sand she insisted they carry from the first day of travel. She had said to Welcome, "This is part of my bidding to you," advice that he understood all the way to the root of its compass.

That night, around the campfire, the wagon master, Big Buck Mulligan, leading his third train west, said, "Welcome, I was surprised that your faithful old Brown Bess was not already loaded and your woman, MM there, had to load it for you. Something to that?"

"Sure is, Buck, It's all her doing 'cause she knows if I see a rabbit on the loose, any old time, I'll go ahead an' keen-eye knock it down, an' she don't want none of that."

"She worried about alarmin' sleepin' Indians, Welcome?"

"No sir, Buck, 'cause she's allus sayin' a caught rabbit is easier done on the fire than a shot rabbit, an' I swear that's one holy truth comin' clear out of her mouth."

Buck, being a most pleasant man, roared with laughter, and kept it up for a while, enough for those gathered to reflect on his way of life, which Welcome knew down to the nitty gritty, as he'd say if asked. "In the first place, now on his third train being led west, Buck accepts no money for his completion, but whenever the train arrives at a final place and starts to build or add to a place already with some good roots, the men of the train have to build, inside of a year, a place for him and hold it for him, as all agreed right up at the front end of the connections."

And wouldn't you know, from what we know that Welcome kept up with, "that Big Buck Mulligan would end up having four places of his own west of the two big rivers, all that coming to a man whose folks were routed from their home in Ireland and had to move from their beloved homeland to new expectations. Now he has places for his own children, come what may. That's a man getting ready for the whatever, if you were to ask me," as Welcome would finish his history of Big Buck Mulligan, whenever he had a mind to do so, or was asked by a fellow traveler or townsman when they got to Hallows Hill, closer to the Pacific Ocean than any of them ever dreamed.

But that's getting ahead of the story of MariaMary and Bill I and Bill II and Welcome Walcott himself, as said, right out of the North of Scotland.

The boys were 8 almost 9, the pair of them, the wagons rolling through Navajo and Apache country, and then Pueblo territories and ending up in a splendid valley of dreams just after passing several Chumash tribe villages and as close to the grand Pacific Ocean as they'd ever be.

They had settled down, built a home, shared in the building of Big Buck's new place, and the "twins" beginning to ask questions about themselves, looking at each other, seeing the closeness as skins matched each other's skin. They each admitted the curiosity had started with several visits from a most friendly Indian of the local tribe whose name was Falcon's Edge. The Indian, very attentive to the boys, once said to Bill II, "You're the one I watch with the special eye of the falcon from his high reach. You are more Indian than your brother, Bill I. I have seen it with my own eyes and the eyes of a falcon from that high rest. I am never wrong in these matters. I should ask about these considerations. I should ask your father but some spirit says I should ask your mother."

Falcon's Edge's face, right arm only, and one thigh, carried secret designations of traceability that he would not discuss, simply saying, "I carry the legends of my people. I have seen how your people carry their legends in books that are too heavy to carry even for men bigger than I am. Tomorrows will be added here," as he pointed to his bared arm and bared thigh, neither yet bearing any lore or legend, room enough for all the stories that were to come in his time, at least.

He finally asked Welcome Walcott if he could speak to his wife, and Walcott agreed on the spot, having built up some esteem for the decorated, historical Indian. "Of course you can speak to her and I suppose it is about the boys. Am I right, Falcon's Edge? Do I see that in your face as I have seen it before, that same quizzical look?"

The first smile crossed the face of Falcon's Edge, as if some interior agreement had also been reached. "We are more alike, Walcott. It is like the boys. Am I right there?"

Walcott enjoyed his own smile in return.

MariaMary looked up from her work in a small yard garden, ripe with green leaves, as Falcon's Edge hailed her. "Walcott has given me permission to talk to you about the boys, as he and I have similar feelings, I believe, as do those boys of yours, your twins."

The appellation of *twins* came quickly to MariaMary, who set her tools on a rock, brushed herself off, and said, "It has been a long while since I thought of such a reference, Falcon's Edge. I know you come with more than curiosity, for both boys have informed me of your words and feelings about them."

One hand went to her forehead, as she said, "Oh, where do I start?"

"From the heart of the beginning." Deep concern came into his voice with those words. "I do not pry into affairs, only seeing some kind of light that comes back to me when the boys are with me. It is continual and almost holy."

"Well, it's about time. I'll call the boys." Their names sang in the air and they appeared as if they had been waiting for this moment for a long time, each kneeling quietly beside the garden rock.

The woman of the family looked at all three kneeling near her. "Years ago, after Bill I was born, and near the end of that same year, promise of snow in the air, we came to an Indian village burned to the ground, each and every teepee, and the silence was deafening, and the stink of bodies quite horrific. Then, after a hurried look about, we heard the cry of a child, the cries somewhat muffled, perhaps distant or somehow covered or protected. He was hard to find at first, the sound of his cries sort of hollow, and finally we found him stuffed inside a hollow log at the edge of the village, a village of the Iroquois, perhaps a few westerly days ride from Boston. We cleaned him up, fed him, and I comforted him as his mother must have done, hugging him to my breast, treating him to any milk left in me. I loved him at that moment as I loved my own son, and now I had two sons, I thought to myself."

She gathered the two boys into her arms, tears flooding her face, "My boys," she cried, "My boys."

They hugged her back, like two youngsters called home for a surprise, while a wise Sachem of a sort looked on in deepest appreciation, and Welcome Walcott, not very far away from the gathering, managed to say to himself, "Finally Bill I and Bill II have it squared away for each other, and it's off my mind forever."

He threw the Indian, Falcon's Edge, the first salute he had ever thrown to anybody in this life of his, in this world of the wide open West.

The argument started in the Cows' Moon Saloon in the town of Stream's Edge on the River Moses, a small stream of sorts in East Texas, when two ranchers of the area tossed barbs and curses at one another over now forgotten issues, but set the groundwork for later. Generally such spouts are about ownership or lines of demarcation, or natural barriers or lines that should settle most arguments by long-known local sightings. (Never about women; they wouldn't allow it.)

Ownership, thus, was settled by loudest voice, first to declare a line, a line marked by natural terrain, or a really visible and normal edge of discussion: a river, a stream, "a piss puddle" someone once uttered in disgust when his declaration was cast off with disdain by listeners, on-lookers, a half-drunk barkeep steeped in his own responsibilities.

The two arguers, combatants, were Wedge McMurry and Sledge Hanswick, so named early on by the same neighbors who still gathered at the Cows' Moon, all older than the two contestants in the current argument over land lines, ownership, where the river really splits, as seasonal changes sometimes forced slight but important alterations in one boundary that may leapfrog subtle or large changes down the line, be it so called as so agreed by at least two or more people.

That young pair, each born to be big and tall men, full-chested, powerful, quick of hand and fist, and unafraid of just about anyone and anything that came their way on foot, paw or horseback. They, in turn admired by the older set, were often pitted against one another for joy's sake of on-lookers, bettors, fight fans before the term came into being. Each of the growing boys agreed to such bouts, early and often with overhand swings and jaw-crunches of the first class, and each had their own gallery of fans, gallery gods too, also before that term came along in conversations, spats, "more troubles brewed up on the spot."

Sledge and Wedge, as it was, went into their twenties, became ranch owners within a year of each other when both fathers fell to rustlers' intrusions a bare month apart. They shared their sorrows and their sufferings as good friends, and went about their business of becoming ranch owners, cowmen to the core, each angling to outgrow the other with similar sorrows but no vindictiveness at the start of the new holdings.

It can be seen that their early encounters, bolstered by others for joy, came upon them with a need to overcome the other at any and every level of competence, measurement, increase, or social standing, such as it was in those days.

This day in May of 1861 found them in the midst of the latest argument at the Cows' Moon Saloon when a lone cowboy rammed through the saloon doors screaming, "Someone blew up the mid-course dam of the River Moses and the water's taken a new course heading down this way. No tellin' what it's gonna do when it gets here! It'll run those property lines all over Hell!"

He threw his arms in the air and yelled out, "Get me a drink 'cause I won't know who owns what! You can't reckon with the wreckin'." His laughter was far beyond instant thoughts of most men in the Cows' Moon Saloon, most of them seeing an instant confrontation, already tasting the blood of the matter.

Silence swung through the crowded room like an odd night was happening, almost a darkness of clarity, of what could and would happen to property lines once declared hard and fast. The barkeep kept shaking his head the way amazement shows itself in human reflection, but much of that amazement is what surged in the crowded room, what played out for the future not yet in sight ... but coming in a hurry, like anger and deprivation, land loss, shrinkage of property or sudden riches in the same vein, fist-tossing, blood-letting, false justice chasing after the good reckoning, thumbs up on shootings, reparation, exactitude by the acre regained in a damnable hurry before stakes were hammered into new property lines.

The whole essence of wide open space was at times illusionary, the way the grass, the rolling hills of plains and neatness of meadows, the fertile prairies as far as many eyes could see, once free territory for all, might have room for a whole new crib for all of Earth to replant itself with another chance at settling down again, taking another chance, in spite of those who coveted it the most.

Opposite sides were already drawn for the coming encounter, or so it seemed.

"No foolin' with the toolin'," as they might and often did say up along the River Moses, all of East Texas at attention for any and all changes in the landscape, the ownership and the destiny of those two ranches, cattle-marked with the *luck of the Irish* or *Swede Sweetness*, the *Irish in Public (I/P)* or the other end of the argument, the *Swedish Nightmare (S/N)*. The brands were known all over Texas and all neighboring states and territories in all directions, the brand name carried by tongue and tale by like-bred travelers from the old countries across the new land of America. Some might talk of "recovery" or of "theft." Each version in the employ of men who thrived on ownership to the last end, for the "big bite," strong enough to make a grab whenever the chance came along, the way accidents happen, the way fate makes a move, the way luck has a hand in things.

Wedge McMurry moved first from his seat at a poker table. "It's all your doing, Sledge. You either planted dynamite by yourself or paid to have it done!" Anger rode in his face as if he was being strangled, his cheeks puffed and balloon-like, his teeth bared, his eyes lit by fire of a blue code. All his body said he had been robbed by a maneuver he had not even dreamed of, the course of the river being split, being diverted, cutting edges at new outlines, new parameters. It was all falling apart from a good bond.

He started across the room at Sledge Hanswick, shouting, "I ought to kill you for this. You've screwed up everything we had kept in line. We agreed on the river. We said it was okay for both of us. You shook my hand on it."

Partway across the room he halted, looked about him at the audience of men they had known most of their lives and said, in a swift change, "Let's face it, Sledge, whoever did it or arranged it, to get at us for sure, is most likely in this saloon right now."

The silence rode over every face in the room, a testimony about that declaration, and the action that promised to follow.

Wedge's eyes roamed over the saloon full of old friends, hardy cowmen from the first word of dawn, "Go", "Get done", "Do it before somebody else does it." Most every man in the room moved with those words on his mind, being born with them in their hearing.

He found the center of his mind, the track he wanted to take.

"I'll explain my meaning with these words," he managed in a moderate tone, a deep breath taken for his broad chest.

"You and I handle cards in a different manner, Sledge. You always concentrate on the cards. They mean everything to you when they're dealt; everything, to the end of the world. But, I say now and forever, cards dealt to me, all cards, are *or should be* accidents, they are plain all-out *accidents*, almost illusions. I pay little attention to them. Instead, I pay strict attention to the hands and the eyes of those players at the table with me, at nobody else. I study their hands above the table, and their eyes above their hands, as well as their twitches, their quick moves, the nerves, the giveaways free for the taking. They tell me a lot that's never said but hangs in their minds like they'll never let go of them, but damned it, man, they're all loose in this room right now."

"If anyone can benefit by any change in property lines on the stream, or the new slant or angle of it, it's someone else who also has property on the line, and that's a very nervous man at this table with me right now, scared to death about discovery more than what his cards are going to do for him, his hands at a jingle-jangle, his fingers loose as tail feathers on the back end of a horse, I swear his hands feeling like gloves have been glued to his palms."

Blackcat Spoffard, no first name ever known, never used in or outside of these games, a thin and dark-set man with mustache and curly black hair down his back, was suddenly stiff in his seat, as if dynamite was expelling its foul residue from his very person, a sharp and acidic waste emanating from his skin, wide and foul as a pigpen at a farm site, the giveaways of giveaways. Everything but the *big boom* in the transition.

Of course, shaken wide awake from his soft dreaming at cards, *Blackcat* leaped from his chair to make a break from the room, but Wedge had a solid hand on him before he could take a step or utter a breath.

"Your cards are all dealt for you, *Blackcat*. You can't get away from this hand, that's for damned sure." He held the other hand in the air. "This other hand in this deal is gonna be for justice and for punishment. That's my promise to all of you gents here and especially to this rat of a man."

He swung a solid fist at *Blackcat*, letting it miss by a hair's edge. The dynamiter collapsed in terror and fright, not a blow struck for justice, no room left for more forgiveness, as all was cast for his future in the town, if there was any future to be had beyond this day.

With the ease of a giant, Wedge McMurry picked up the unconscious man and dumped him in the dust of the road. That was the last anybody in Stream's Edge ever saw of him.

The rider stood in his stirrups to get a better look down into the valley where a ranch spread its arms near as wide as the valley floor, all the while nodding his head at every positive presentation ... house, barns, corrals, two horseshoe pits, a solid thus permanent outdoor fireplace signifying some mostly good times he figured.

It didn't take him long to seek a job at this ranch.

"So you're Nathan *Nat* Knowles, 22 year old cowpoke looking for another job, six years on six ranches or drives in your past few years." said the owner, George Bee. "Once I was a marshal but got tired of it and the ugly company I had to keep. Tell me some of those places you worked and why you left them. That's quite a change-over for a young stud. You that restless or looking for something special?" His face flooded with wonder. He looked with an affirmative gaze, and honest satisfaction, at the situation around him, a kind of conscious acceptance of things as they were. His conscious smile was significant, and the knowledge spanned between the two men in quick recognition.

The young cowpoke said, his voice coming back to George Bee without any added inflection, no spice or color in the mix; just plain fact. "With Harland Jackson at the Topeka spread before he moved to his new river place. Still there from what I heard. Then there was Spooky Shadock in Bristletoe, and Mark Waltham at the Circle W. Places like that. New slots of work, no pushing or shoving, just movin' along."

"Satisfies me, son," Bee said, putting out his hand. "You've been on some good spreads, with some mighty good folk. Welcome to another, to Beehive. Foreman's name is Quick 'n' Straight Smith, honest to gawd, way he introduces hisself to any and all. I like and trust him, he's almost old as me and been on some of the same road." He paused and added, "'Course, that ain't forever."

It sounded as much a declaration as a warning, which Nat Knowles heard on the early syllables. Straight talk had a way of settling spats to small wars in the making.

As he turned to seek out the foreman for bunkhouse quarters, rules of the ranch, sundry other duties of the job, Bee added, "One other thing I might advise, son. I have a daughter, not yet 18, been her own woman since I lost my wife half a dozen years ago. Name's CarlaBee all together the way she likes it, of her own mind like I said and out of bounds unless she smiles at you." The wink might have been an eye opener, or a gesture with good will hanging on it.

He looked over Nat Knowles one more time and decided out loud, "She might find this interesting." He nodded a few times, the way older men nod with affirmation and not guesswork, and said, "Might she will."

His head rolled in a slight indication, as though a determination was en route.

Nat Knowles felt the welcome on the spot, even as he looked about the ranch for a spur of color, for the flash of a yellow or pink shirt, for a horse prettied up beyond the barn, and suddenly understood he was looking for the wrong things the way his new employer had laid them out, plain as a brand worked into place, as good as land or law.

When he passed the side of the ranch house, he caught a glimpse of a pretty face moving away from a window, as though he had already been checked out by a one-way girl at her own leisure. The feeling shone in his face and a sense of guesswork walked with him, the sweet curiosity a sweet woman can raise in so many easy ways without even half trying.

A guess said it wouldn't be too long before they met, figuring curiosity worked both ways between men and women, between young folks full of energy and imagination, the old drawing power between folks that he had heard from old timers up and down the trail, from those who'd been there and back, as it was often summed around a kindly trail fire.

Knowles realized he was a listener from whisper to wail, could tell what people were like from their talk, as well as their silence, was often right on the mark; how would it be with this CarlaBee?

She was beside him in a rush, saying, "I'm going to follow you around. I'll be everywhere you go. Since I was 12 I've been waiting for my man to come along, my best love, my true love, and you are the best one I have seen in almost six years, the only one really. I promise you and myself I will be my own woman when I come to 18. My father knows it. All his hired hands know it, every one of them he's hired over the years, including you. There's no mystery to it. I am going to claim you as mine. You will be my first and only lover out there in some secret place we'll come to know every once in a while as 'our place.' I bring that with me though I haven't even found it yet myself. We are going to find it, our place and heaven of celebration, for our first time and for our forever. Your piece of the big pie because someday, like Pa says, this place will be mine and, of course, yours. You can bet on it for that first place whenever it comes up; the first one, the only one, and the sooner you realize it, the sooner it gets done ... once I am 18."

CarlaBee wound herself up, for the first time ever he saw her face flushed with excitement, all phases of it marked with her beauty. "You be ready for me, Nat Knowles; I'll be irresistible, and that's another promise you can dwell on. Think about the way you want me when the time comes."

Her smile, the movements she cast off from her beautiful body almost hidden in colors, the promise loaded into her message, the aura of her selection and presentation, landed atop Nat Knowles like a stick of dynamite had been flung his way like a single target under barrage. Not knowing if it was curse or promise, he was speechless, said nothing in response, but rode off to the balance of his day, his mind loaded with images, with pictures she had created, cast his way, the challenge of a 17 year old owner's daughter soon to be 18, soon to be his.

Cows, horses, riders, the grass itself, faded in and out of his mind, much of that mind occupied otherwise with a host of miracles, coming attractions, events of a lifetime, majesty of thought of a man's thoughts on the very loose, like a whole remuda breaking free of bonding, or a whole vast herd of cattle on the roll. All the possibilities of tomorrow came in a rush, just as if she had spun the whole matter through her mind a hundred times, rehearsed them, corrected them, re-spun them to her ideas of sweet perfection.

He was blushed, overpowered, feeling his visibility and his long secretive self was now exposed, but he was alive, kicking, thinking. "This is a girl, a woman, setting the way, calling the shots at 17, but knowing more than he had ever dreamed about a woman along the long trail, the crowded bars and saloons. Things like this never happen, but I've never met someone like CarlaBee. There's no one in all the west, in all the country, like her and I know she knows that. She made herself that way without a mother for the last six years. A challenge she took on herself. Now it's my turn. It's pointed right at me and nobody else. How the hell do I handle this? Will her father fire me? Will he chase me off? Will he send her away? Oh, that's easy ... if he did, she'd come back in a hurry. She's sure gonna do what she promises."

CarlaBee's birthday came along the way, all hands invited, music and gaiety galore, two bonfires lighting up the area, her dancing, in turn, with a dozen hands that wouldn't once have put a hand on her, though they might have dreamed it or thought it. And her father sitting off to one side, thinking again and again how his wife would love this moment as much as he did, and would most likely dread it at the same instant. Some hands stood fully agape, some in line for her minute though generous favors, some glad the moment had come for the future owner of a most prosperous ranch in hundreds of miles.

Then, the gala in full swing, the moon almost filling up the sky, her having danced with every one of the hired hands, young and old who had stood in line it seems (except for one, of course), she sought out Nat Knowles, her hand touching him on the shoulder while he was talking to another hand twice or three times as old as he was, her face lit with realization, charm, pleasure, and a ferocious kind of intensity as though something had come over her from a long wait.

Her father had raised his hand at the hour of midnight, signifying her birthday had come upon all of them, and then CarlaBee had raised her hand, had touched him for the first time, said, "Dance with me," her voice soft, almost diminutive for the first time, and added, "and then we'll take a ride looking for a secret place out there someplace."

Nat Knowles gulped, the gasp caught in his throat, "Yes,'m," he said, conscious of two things, that she was a raving beauty who had come to him, and she was now 18, and her own woman, as she had promised.

"Your horse is ready. So is mine. Quick 'n' Straight took care of it for me. 'Part of a birthday present' as he said. I think he must have been talking to my Pa too. Seems to know more than any of the hands. At least he's aware of a few things that really count with me. They've been tied off at the back of the big barn, waiting all night for us.

In the bright moonlight and the glow of two fires, the young couple walked away from the gathering, CarlaBee casting one long and serious look at her father sitting with Quick 'n' Straight before she put her hand in the hand of her announced one-love-forever.

In the darkness behind the barn, in the company of two saddled horses, CarlaBee kissed Nat Knowles for the first time. He kissed her back, the revolutions and spirits abounding in each of them. When they finally let go of each other, he lifted her onto her saddle with a whisk of energy, and mounted his own horse.

"You're leading the way, Ma'am," he said.

"From now on it's CarlaBee, or 'my love' or 'darlin', or whatever you want to make of it, but often and sooner each time. I am delirious. I am with my one love forever, as promised when I was 17, but now I'm 18, my own woman, and your own woman. I have no regrets for my waiting, for what I might have put my father through, him without his wife, my mother, all these years of waiting. I am deliciously happy. Now let's go find a happy place for our first celebration."

She led the way out of the barn's darkness into the moonlight of the night, the wide grass drifting off to wherever out in front of them, rolling the way a river does its work, slow at times but full of promise, happy times, wonders by the wagonloads or boatloads, but it was obvious to Nat Knowles that CarlaBee knew exactly where she was going.

Her mount reacted to the spurs as she galloped across the moonlit prairie.

Conversation

The barber Jose Belmonte, from his small shop at the edge of town, first noted the rider coming into Silver Rialto, day at its early start, and wondered where the man might have spent the night, the town a full day's ride from anyplace halfway alive with people. Jose saw a man worn down by a long ride or one driven by need, and thought it might be a needed drink before a solid meal. A lot of that had passed the other side of the glass.

He was pleasantly excited and pleased when the stranger pulled up in front of his shop and tied his horse to the rail.

"Change my appearance if you can, Mr. Barber. Make me a different man. I ain't been in a shop like this in a whole year on the chase." The voice was officious though the body was not; no star on the chest, grubby looking, more like a miner than a cowpoke.

"You a lawman?" Jose said in a quick response full of respect, his face flushed with excitement, figuring Silver Rialto was the final target of a wanted man chased here for part of forever; a "whole year" keeping his mind leaping to guesses. Hopes for success, a quick arrest, an unsuspected citizen worth a year's push across the plains dotted with many towns he'd never been in himself.

"You and me know that, and only us, until the time I tell you my job's done. Keep it in mind, meanin' to yourself and no exceptions allowed. You start cuttin' 'n' trimmin' and I'll tell you why and what for. Deal?" He nodded without hearing a response, as if no response would count in any favor.

"There's more than a few mommas back down the trail who have had their kids killed right in front of them for little reason outside of hate, fear, and whatever makes a man ascared of his life because some kid or his momma has stood up against him. That kind of a lousy punk of a man I've tracked here, right to Silver Rialto. Almost had him a week ago, in Mount Sermon over in the Big Hills. Beat me out of town on a stolen horse while I was waitin' beside his horse for him to mount up. A slippery dude, for sure, ahead of me almost a whole year and me almost sick and tired of it all, but willin' to give it a few more days, hopin' it's here."

"What's he look like, this killer?"

"Big in the saddle. Rides high, a six-footer, yaller hair hangin' in back like it's lookin' for favor, wears a pair of guns on his belt, damned good with them and too good for his own good if I do say so. No name now I know of, but John Collmore at least his birth name. Could call himself anything 'cept a decent man. You seen a man like that? Cut his hair? Swept up after him, Mister Barber?"

71

Jose had big trouble controlling himself and damned near choked on his reply. "Harry Devine he calls himself, I suppose for the time bein'," his Adam's apple jumping in his throat, his hands gone edgy and shaky, appearing like no barber anybody would like to get his hair cut from.

"Still around? When's the last time you saw him? He still wearin' two guns? I allus like to git ready aforehand, as you might know."

Jose worked to get back his breath, which had rushed out of his small frame. "I cut his hair about six times so far. Comes in every week to get that blond hair trimmed. Is real particular about it. Tips me good but don't say nothin' but 'Do it like last time' and means it, like he'd pay me back somethin' awful if I didn't do a good job. Don't know anybody else got that feelin' about his hair."

"That's real interestin' and sounds like my man. This time you get a piece of the reward for your good turn."

"That ain't all," Jose dropped his voice almost to a whisper when he continued, looking around the shop as though someone was looking on, listening in. His breath came back in a rush, but his hands still shaking like no pair of scissors ever found comfort or good use in those fingers.

"Why's that?" The stranger, no name offered yet, tipped his head in marked curiosity as his eyes checked out the interior of the shop, scanned the outsides visible through the window, saw his horse at gainful rest. Little else caught his eye, nothing drew a steady gaze, the small-town silence about them somewhat irritable, unusual.

"He's due here today, Devine is. Told me last time he'd be in this day, Friday, near end of the week, him sparkin' a widow right here in town." He gasped an added cry, "Gawd, she's got two kids hangin' on her skirts, not lettin' go yet. I don't think they're even 10 yet. Neither one. You mean, he hurts kids like that?" His hands shook up to his elbows, for sure.

The pressure in his body, his whole chest caught up in the moment, came at him in a heavy and realistic sensation, shortening his breath, exposing his nerves he believed must be bouncing off the skin of his hands, his neck, especially at the back of his neck. It made him think of a couple of bandits and killers he had seen get hanged by the neck right there outside his place of business, the rope grabbed tight by their own bodies moving in the air like they were nothing more than feathers in the wind. Not their arms moving them, not their hands pushing at air, but even the smallest breath of air in control of them, them no longer controlling anything but a hush to the edges of town, a silence, a still crowd in a motionless circle around the hastily constructed gallows of every execution, mouths open, at the very edge of the crowd a lawman walking away from the act of law like he had nothing more to do with it, hands clean of it all. Day and deed done, dollar earned one more time. Nothing's like success, and more so further west one goes these days.

The visitor and inquisitor said, "Gets back at their mommas the worst way he can. Yup, you got a chunk of reward money comin' for all this news. Best tell me the lady's name and where she lives in case I gotta pay a visit there." His eyes were still on the saloon across the road, a few customers already having entered the premises, the barkeep at attention, day at hand but night a long ways off.

"Name's Mildred Greenspent. Lives in a small cabin just at the far side of town, t'other way, t'other end of the road, like you was goin' to California or Oregon or the damned Pacific Ocean itself. He spends some time every other night, I hear, over there, like it's his strike. I heard that from some other customers come in on pay days or loaded with a flush of gamblin' money."

Sometimes Jose spoke out of the side of his mouth as if some ornery soul was listening to him, maybe him talking too much, his head swinging slowly around in a new search for old trouble kicking up because of his own mouth running up enough trouble for a month or two, or for a whole year. The thought came to him that he might even have to move further west, to another town. He'd done it before, getting to Silver Rialto the same way, on the move, making a break as if he was a criminal in his own way.

"That's interestin', Jose. My name, if it comes up for any reason, is Dever Drumm with two M's if you will. I'm the marshal out of Steakhill, just so's you at least know the whole story, or most of the parts. When's he due for a trimmin'?"

"My Gawd, Marshal, he's bound to come in this mornin'. Could be any time." He went to the window and looked both ways of the single road into and out of Silver Rialto. "He even might come from the saloon, even this early. Came that way a couple of times, otherwise it's from her house, like I said. From Mildred Greenspent's house and her two kids." He paused and added, "Oh, Gawd," like a bad deed had been kicked loose again.

"Well, clean me up quicker'n you figured and I'll sit like I'm visitin' you awhile, shootin' the breeze about nothin' at all and every thin' else important. Okay?" His voice had lowered to just above a whisper, and Jose didn't realize it had calmed his own self down to a slow walk, so to speak.

The marshal, his eyes on the saloon across the road, said, "He leave his guns on when he sits that chair?"

"Sure does. Draws them across his lap kind of, for comfort and keepin' them free for use. Have to tell you that, Marshal, keeps them free for use, and right in his lap like I said."

He shook his head again, as though he once more thought he'd said too damned much to a man he'd never seen before and might never see again.

Dever Drumm spoke in a soft manner, but words with an edge on them. "Better not call me 'Marshal' again, and get used to not sayin' it. Best call me Rex, somethin' short and easy, Yep, Rex sounds good for now if our friend comes in like he's supposed to."

"Oh, he'll be in for sure, Rex," and he said the name sitting on his lips, in his mouth for ten seconds, like he'd used it a hundred times. "Always comes early, right from her place or the saloon, never know which, as I said a few times." It sounded firm and heavy for the first time, the quick preparation working already, his comfort showing in place, confidence working, allied with the lawman sitting there with him.

Jose jumped when the marshal asked, "This him comin' now, from the saloon, big as hell he is."

"Oh, Gawd, yes, that's him, Marshal."

"Rex it is Jose. Rex. Best well prepare yourself not to blow apart whatever comes down on us. It might pay off for you and for me. This is a real bad dude comin' our way.

When the door opened and Harry Devine as he was known, came into the barbershop, he checked out Drumm with a quick glance and said to Jose Belmonte, "Who you got for company, Jose? He ahead of me? I told you I was comin' this mornin', didn't I? You gotta remember stuff like that."

"Oh, I didn't put him ahead of you, Harry. I was just shootin' the breeze with Rex here, Rex Smith from back east a way. Rex, this is Harry Devine, 'nother cowpoke like yourself."

The two men of the west nodded at each other in their curt manner. "Where you from, Smitty, and what brings you to Silver Rialto?"

"The name itself," said the marshal in a matter-of-fact tone, sounding as if he had said it a hundred times in the same way. "Sparkles a little, it does, Better than Boxford or Cliffside or Cowville itself. I just heard it once and said to myself, 'I want to go see that place' and here I am."

The wanted man smiled and said, "You didn't say where you were from as he sat down in the barber chair and swung his pair of guns across his lap so they sat clearly visible, attainable, dangerous as any pair of pistols ever looked.

He looked down once, and when he looked up the marshal's gun was pointed directly at his chest. "I'm Marshal Dever Drumm from Steakhill, on your tail a long while, John Collmore, and was just sittin' here with Jose waitin' for you to show up. You make one move and you're dead."

His gun didn't waver a speck, steady as a steel rail, his voice changed into the voice of office, when he said, "Jose, go behind the man and pull each pistol from his lap, nice and easy, sure and easy just the way you know I mean it. Don't throw them, but put them into that bucket in the corner."

"John Collmore, I arrest you for multiple murders on your way here, and on your way back to make payment. I'm done with my talkin'."

It was done. Collmore, wrists bound in chains, hoisted onto a horse and starting back the way both men had come, went to doom and more silence than he had ever known.

From high on the ridge of a Teton Range "middle-mountain," as he called the lesser landscape minions of the Wyoming territory, Lucas Woodcock heard first, and then saw, the west-bound stagecoach at a standstill, as the 4-horse team reared amid shrill cries of desperation and fear.

Somewhere in the cover of the scaly backdrop, a mountain lion roared its threats, shrill screams, deathly intentions. The cat, sounding as large as its roars, dominated the passage of the stagecoach on a regular run through the lower Tetons.

And Lucas saw the lady in a red outfit sprawled on the top of the coach, her legs spread as if ready to leap, reap revenge, a huntress already, in vogue red. Or gone higher to escape trouble.

He hadn't seen a woman in all the summer months and was sure it would be a testy introduction when appropriate.

His single round, aimed into a dark spot of a wall, shook loose a mountain lion, probably at its feed of a slain goat or sheep.

The lion broke free of its meal, roared its defiance once more, and disappeared through darker crags of the late afternoon.

Lucas, offhandedly said, "See you later, Willie." There was a definite touch of pity in his voice and a somewhat tender understanding of the animal's own natural conduct, and calling the cat by a familiar name said they were at least acquainted. The natural elements abounding about the mountain man had long been expected and respected by the hunter on his own terms of survival. He and those animals shared the world's bounty.

A sudden image tore into Lucas' mind, knowing the coach would stop the night at the Dead Mule Station at the end of the valley. After a few more tough and exaggerated turns, the coach would be in sight of the station.

Lucas hadn't seen Muley Manuel in months, the Mexican transplant telling Lucas once that he loved horses, mountain lions, wolves, bear cats, goats, sheep, even an occasional rattler "as long as they ain't at the same dinner table with me, eh, *senor*."

And he reminded himself that he hadn't seen a woman in twice that long, and especially one specimen in an all-red outfit *"right outta some store winda."*

He was due.

He fired his second shot into the cliff-face away from the coach and the driver waved back, partial recognition in action.

With an urgency, Lucas' down-hill trek was twice his normal speed; the woman in red an incomplete target of his thoughts, but she was also a persistent cuss, appearing again and again in the back of his mind, in the middle of it, in the wide spaces he allowed up front for probably a most buxom lady. The mountains have more ways than one to twist a man's mind – even a solid hunter like Lucas Woodcock.

There was no doubt she was worth the hurry.

Dusk eventually brought to his gaze the dim light of a window at the station. He imagined the team of horses stabled for the night, the driver and the shotgun rider near their needed sleep in a comfortable corner, and old Muley talking his endless chatter with *his* woman in red. He didn't think of her as *Muley's* woman, not by the healthiest of shots.

With dusk getting deeper, thicker, darker, and less than 100 yards from the station, Lucas, in one breath, swore he could smell the woman in red, as if she was nestled in the safety of his arms. Deeply he breathed, almost taking her all the way home. The proof of it was Muley's dog, not having seen Lucas for months, who came near him wagging his tail at Lucas' arrival where the road hits a level approach to the station. Common ground, regardless of time's measure swayed each one.

Not 30 yards from the station cabin, as if he was suddenly called to duty, the dog uttered a loud howl of warning, to let all know company was coming.

Lucas patted him on the head and said, "Quiet, Jackson, they'll know company's coming soon enough, and I'm urgent to meet them." He almost said, "That lady in red, star of the show, any show," he'd bet. The new, different, delicate, fine and fragile air settled in his lungs as though it was coiled in a sweet syrup.

Muley met him at the open door, the two coachmen standing behind him with pistols in hand, the lady in red, buxom indeed, said, "Muley here said a mountain man named Lucas had done the trick for us out there, might have kept us from going over the side of the road and down the mountain the quick way. You that Lucas, mountain man?"

"I guess I am, Ma'am," Lucas replied, his eyes in a ready sweep of beauty and appreciation in one glance. "Couldn't help not helping, seeing you up on the rack holding on for a sure dear life. Yes, Ma'am, I'm Lucas Woodcock, at your service."

"I have to admit, Lucas, I must owe you all I own. My name's Marla, short for Marla Carla Columbiana." The slightest stance movement inside that surge of red beauty was clear as if written on the blackboard at a country school. Twice she sent that shivered signal, twice Lucas read it.

Muley interjected the introduction. "I knew you didn't come with dinner on your shoulder, Lucas, cuz Marco would've said so." He patted the hound on the head. "He always like you, Lucas, from first meeting, now smell you a mile off." He added, "Like now," an open observation of his own, saying he was aware of body language, the pros and cons of it for men living alone in the mostly wild part of the world where women in red outfits didn't climb hills or rocky knobs or play tag on quiet days.

Marla said, openly, fully inquisitive, interested, "Do you live in a place like this, out here in this country?" She held out one hand as if measuring Muley's log cabin, 20 feet by 20 feet, 3 bunks on one wall practically on top of each other, one wall a solid stone fireplace with extended stone floor burnt black forever. A separate bunk bed hung on another wall. A table of rough-hewn boards sat in the middle of the cabin with two pairs of chairs made from similar hewn material. One shuttered window faced easterly, from where the coach had come.

She kept looking around as she talked, as she obviously measured, as does a woman looking for a work counter, storage space, privacy, other facilities obviously outside between the cabin and the small three-sided barn where the horses were tethered. The odors of a fast meal were fading fast, and her secret application of a bit of perfume staking its own claim.

"Oh, no, Marla," Lucas said, inhaling, as if her name made his mouth delicious, his eyes lighting up, circled by a growth of hair mostly blond, mostly long, on his head and chin. "I live in a cave, in the side of a mountain with lots of cover above me, protective cover." He pointed to the cabin roof, at a one-way steep slant. "I have plenty of comfort, feel secure from scouring animals or those on the hunt. I never get rain or snow in there. Easy to keep warm in cold weather. No leaks, not a one. Two ways in and out. Really a home away from home, that being long gone now, way back east in Tennessee, last seen more'n a dozen years now."

His face showed a solid content for his chosen life, his natural home, his apparent solitude handled with ease.

She was making moves that said things. Lucas was sure of that, not taking his eyes off her, him doing his own measuring, meditating, pleasuring.

"How far is your new home from here?"

Lucas noted she had not called it a cave. "About three hours from here to the foot of the cliff, then a half hour's climb, all of it good exercise for the body."

"Would you like some company going back there this time? I'm serious." That was jammed into the issue to dissuade any negative response. "I look at it this way; I'm on my way from a town I've already forgotten to another one I'll forget just as fast once I leave it, which I most surely will. It comes as a great adventure for me with a real man." Her pursed lips threw him a kiss.

She directed her hand to the two coachmen now fast asleep on the two lowest bunks on the far wall, snores in the air, this day already old and in the folds of memory.

The new couple, for he quickly said yes to the proposal, sat side by side in the rough chairs at the table, Muley and Carlo on their evening check.

Lucas' hand found her hand, lavished it with sweet energy, caught his breath at the touch coming back to him. His eyes closed, and opened suddenly as Marla Columbiana's lips kissed his lips and she nestled against him.

The snoring continued from the bottom bunk on the far wall, a yap was heard from Carlo, Muley coughed before he came back into the cabin to see the couple close as possible.

"Excuse me, *senora, senor*, but my rounds are finish. I will take the top bunk, the empty one there with the coachmen." He was about to snuff out the lone candle on the table, when its glow spread across his face with the expression of an idea already there, the same way other messages might be delivered, had been delivered this very day.

"It comes to me, Muley Manuel, from the heart of hearts in Mexico, that I am now the one and only station master here at the Dead Mule Station on the Reagan Stagecoach Line and that my word is the law of the land and all the mountains of the Tetons near here and this cabin in this wilderness. Do you two agree with me?"

In unison Marla Columbiana and Lucas Woodcock both nodded at the same time and said, "Yes, we do."

All the words thus spoken took on a ceremonial flavor, and Muley Manuel said, in a very serious tone, "Then I announce that you are a man and a wife, and have *el derecho legítimo* to sleep in my bed while I sleep on the top bunk over there."

His smile lit the room up just as he snuffed out the candle.

On the top bunk but mere minutes later, he heard the far cry of a mountain lion followed by the sound of the red dress sliding down past a pair of knees in the darkness.

He was still smiling as he rolled toward sleep, knowing something of what was going on in the small cabin. And even the big man himself, Tim Reagan, owner of the stage line, had no better say in this matter.

Coffee

The grass was brown, the tree line green and the mountain tops white, the highest ones sticking up into the vague, pale sky. Not much at all seemed different in the dawn flash. To the roused cowpoke slipping out of his blanket, it all said, "Coffee to start the day."

But there remained from his sleep the elements of a dream upon which he could not put a finger of clarity. A cloudy, nebulous nothing seemed to hang on, though he could not recall the first inkling of it. Associations, he said to himself, might bring back the gist of the dream. He'd wait on one of those associations coming along with a mind of its own, the way his imagined aroma of coffee held sway.

Thornton Turner, English by birth, traveler by choice, cowpoke by need, enjoyed the sun getting stronger. He placed a few stones in a small net-like canvas bag and hitched it to a length of rope when he spotted a dead tree. The dead tree stood like a bleached flagpole at the edge of the tree line with sunlight reflecting on it. Dead and still standing, he thought, and found admiration for the tree, his mind working in its odd way, yanking him alert at the strangest times, seeing more than others might see in an image, in an object. For him the tree had purpose: upright it provided fuel, on the ground it would rot away, back to earth, useless to him but not the worst of outcomes, enriching the Earth once again.

Pulling his horse to a stop under the tree, he heaved the net up toward one limb on the tree. The heavier net swung over the limb and fell about six feet below the limb on the other side. Then he looped the rope around the section above the net, twisted it tightly and pulled the limb down out of the tree. It crashed down in its bleached-out state, like a gift of ivory for the cowpoke wanting his coffee. The Indians identified kindling obtained this way as squaw pine.

With the kindling gathered he had the makings for a good cup of coffee – the coffee pack in his saddlebag with dry matches, and now kindling set up for a fire. Soon he'd have the cup he had been thinking of through half the night, but dared not light a fire in the dark; he had seen Indian activity earlier on the day before. He was not sure if they were friendly or not, though they had not appeared to be a war party.

In a patch of bare ground, the earth with a busy red tone in it, he arranged a few stones he'd found at the tree line, started a fire, put his three-cup coffeepot near the flames.

The aroma of brewing coffee filled the air. It whet his appetite, although he had little food in his saddlebag, a piece of jerky, which he generally disliked, eating it for survival. He shoved the jerky into his pocket.

All the contrasts around him seemed too mixed to be discernible, though some stood apart, perhaps the real and the unreal. He fought to bring back a dream from his night. Some part of it was trying to say "peril" to him or "danger." That's all he could find from the dream.

He had just about finished the second cup of coffee, heady with morning's aroma, when he heard a baby cry from the within the tree line.

That was his dream sound; a crying baby, the peril, the danger; for him, he wondered, or for the baby?

He looked off to the tree line when the cry came again, this time as though the cry was quickly muffled. He pictured a hand placed over a small mouth. He thought of a mother in peril, frightened of being discovered by the cries of what she was trying to protect. Incongruity hit him as the picture stayed at the back of his head.

Images passed through Turner, a whole slew of them in rapid fire, like a salvo of sorts. With his pistol in one hand and the cup of coffee in the other, he walked toward the tree line, heard the cry again, a short, mouth-covered cry, and found a young Indian woman holding an infant. No one else was in the area when he looked around, seeking someone in hiding, fearing enticement or entrapment.

He approached the woman, saw fear sitting in her eyes, and felt sympathy for the infant in her arms. He held his hand up in the universal signal of peace, of friendship, of no harm being harbored within him. With a slow motion, he put away his pistol and then offered the woman the cup of coffee, the aroma still alive in the air. He saw her inhale the aroma as it stayed buoyant in the air about them. The woman did not reach for the cup. Tewksbury placed it on the ground in front of her as the baby cried again, and then he stepped back. She stuck a finger in the cup, tasted the coffee on it, then stuck the finger in the cup again and into the baby's mouth. The baby suckled at her finger. She took a sip of the coffee, dipped a finger again for the baby, gave it to him, and drank again.

She smiled at Turner. He found her a most beautiful woman, young, dark-eyed, black-haired, the rising sun finding elegance, and a worry, in her cheeks, on her face. Her dress was Sioux. A dress of deerskin adorned in several places with teeth from an animal, claws, and rows of beads in a splash of color. She wore the dress with distinction and charm, not parading herself but aware of being in the presence of a kind man, a kind white man with pale green eyes she was not familiar with and made her stare at them, blond hair that fell well below his ears and the color of his shirt.

Turner, trying to find out what he could when she did not answer any of the questions he tossed at her, offered the image of a baby suckling at a mother's breast. She nodded. He turned away and he could hear the baby drawing deeply, as if the coffee had whet its appetite. For a few minutes Turner stayed that way, letting privacy have the hand.

The woman said something in her language that was unknown to Turner, and he turned to face her. She put a finger to her mouth, then her hand. He found a piece of jerky in his pocket and offered it to her. She chewed rapidly, looking down at the baby still at her breast, then looking back at Turner, the smile more radiant on her face.

Still curious about her being alone, and wondering how she had gotten here in this place with no horse in sight, he drummed his fingers on a piece of wood. She understood the imitated sound of hoof beats immediately, and tossed one hand abruptly to one side and grabbed her shoulder and hugged the baby. He understood her as telling him she had fallen from her horse and had hurt her shoulder as she protected the baby. He noticed a bruise on her forehead and figured she had run into a low hanging limb of a tree.

Why she was alone bothered him, and arose the possibility that braves from her tribe would be looking for mother and child.

Turner made triangles of his hands joined at the fingertips and moved them into separate places in a steady pace. Her nod said she understood he was asking about her village, and her eyes lit up with emotion as she swept one hand in a continuous motion. Turner took that to mean her man or her village had forced her departure from their village.

"Oh, my," he said, "what could she have done?"

She put her hand over her heart, shook her head and said angry words in a quick mouthful, and hugged the baby closer.

The mother's instinct was seen in its rarest form by the cowboy. He took her by the hand, patted the baby with his other hand and led her to the side of the fire. She drank the last cup of coffee as Turner saddled his horse and placed several stones on the few sticks yet burning. Smoke drifted into the air of early morning. He mounted his horse, put his hands down for the baby, lifted the now silent one aloft, and then helped her mount the horse to sit right behind him. He passed the infant back to its mother.

The trio rode off into the rising sun, riding off to the nearest spread, which was Charlie Peabody's Triple P, PPP on a line, and Charlie's wife Priscilla, her too from Dorsetshire in the old country and a dear woman with half a dozen children of her own. Help for the mother and child would come with warmth from the Peabodys.

As he rode Turner often looked behind him for signs of any riders, Indian or otherwise. He agreed that he'd be hard pressed to let such a woman go off by herself in any situation, under any circumstance. The image of Priscilla Peabody hugging a child once more came to him repeatedly.

They were about a mile from the Triple P spread when he saw the Indian riding down from a cluster of trees, urging his horse to run faster, screams in his voice and a rifle waving overhead in one hand.

Turner felt the girl cringe against his back, utter a helpless sound, and start to shake.

Turner did not rush off. He dismounted in a hurry, drew his rifle from the saddle sheath, aimed over the saddle where he had positioned the rifle … and brought the Indian to a surprising halt. He sat his horse about 100 yards off apparently waiting for Turner to fire at him.

Turner held his fire as the Indian woman uttered more fearful sounds and clutched the baby tighter against her bosom.

Turner still held his fire and the Indian still sat in place.

After 10 minutes or so, and after waving his rifle in the air and screaming in his language, the brave rode off into the cluster of trees and was not seen again.

The trio was greeted with joy and curiosity by the Peabodys, with Priscilla the first off her porch, a morning coffee in her hand. She handed the cup to Turner and said, "What do we have here, Thorn? I haven't seen you in weeks and you show up with a woman and child. Are they hurt? Hungry? Are they in danger? Are we? Is the child yours?" She reached for the baby and the Indian girl passed the child to her and slid off the horse.

Turner dismounted as Charlie Peabody reached to shake hands. "Where'd you find them, Thorn?"

"Out on the grass. I think she was ushered from her village and one brave came on us as we rode back here. I was on line duty for Griswold, for whom I am now working."

"He come at you, that lone Indian?" Peabody said.

"He gave it a try," Turner answered, "but when I dismounted and steadied a rifle on him from about 100 yards, he wouldn't come any closer. He fully understood I had him straight on."

"He bail out then?" Peabody was nodding at a picture in his mind, seeing the scene out on the prairie, Turner at heroics.

The two men kept talking as Priscilla Peabody ushered the Indian woman off to the porch, still cradling the baby in her arms, cooing to the infant, finding an old happiness she sadly missed. Pouring a cup of coffee for the woman, she pointed to bread and jam on the small table.

"They'll get along, won't they," Turner said as he and Peabody stood apart from them in the ranch yard.

"If she's Sioux, that girl, they will," Peabody said, "'cause Prissy speaks some Sioux if you didn't know. It's like a hobby with her. She's good at that kind of stuff. Picks it up early and easy-like. I sense that you would too, if bent to it. You folks had some good education before you came this way. And I'm damned glad both of you made the trip. I'll tell you, Thorn, when you dismounted out there and took the best aim, he understood you were not a runner. He most likely has run down a few runners in his time. This turn of yours put him in his place. He understood you and what you meant. That's good thinking, Thorn." He shook his head, smiled broadly and patted Turner on the back, saying, "When are you coming to work for me?"

"Oh, Charlie, you know that would spoil a perfect relationship with the lady from Dorsetshire and I surely don't want that to transpire." He laughed as he said it, his relaxation into rhyme, and so did Peabody, knowing the inflection and the full meaning of comfort.

The two of them spun about as Priscilla spun out a few words in Lakota Sioux, and offered her quick translations for the men. *"Taŋyáŋ yahí."* And over her shoulder offered, "Welcome." Then she said, *"Táku eníčiyapi he?"* and explained to the men, "What is your name?" And added, to the Indian woman, *"Akhé eyá yo,"* and to the men, "Say again."

The use of the Sioux language moved along between the women in jerks and starts on the porch, the Indian taking the food offered, smiling at the baby asleep in the arms of the older woman, finding an unknown comfort building around her.

Priscilla Peabody was at her best, mother, friend, and confidant.

Choosing a break in the conversation between the two men, Priscilla Peabody qualified it all from the porch, in a voice filled with satisfied curiosity, "Her name is Two Stars Shining and her baby's name is Small Star. It's a girl. *Numra wicahpi ojaja* and *Cistila wicahpi*. That's who they are. They were ousted from their village by a drunken husband, name of Bear Claw. He's the one came at you out there on the grass and she knows he'll come back at you. But she says adamantly that she will not be going back there."

And as if she could move the mountain herself, and the whole Sioux Nation, Priscilla Peabody looked directly at the two men and said, "Not if I can help it."

Her grin was as broad as Charlie Peabody had seen since the last visit of their eldest daughter, all the way from St. Louis.

All the observations in this matter found resolution. Priscilla Peabody kept firm her stand highlighting the situation. Thornton Turner eventually went work for Charlie Peabody, and Two Stars Shining and Small Star found a home in a cabin on the Triple P ranch with Turner.

And the Englishman from Dorsetshire, Thornton Turner, in one mad day of being shot at too often from long range, as if to drive him into an escape run, dipped into a wadi, dismounted, spurred his horse beyond, and from a slight rise in the wadi made his stand, catching Bear Claw coming over the rise with two other braves, and ended the on-going problem with his rifle after sustaining a bullet in one leg and one in his arm.

In time, Turner became Peabody's foreman and Two Stars Shining became like a daughter to Priscilla Peabody. All parties helped in raising the infant girl to fullness, calling her Star Bright when she had fully grown.

Now and then in those long years following, Turner wondered where he'd be, or Two Stars Shining and her daughter, if he had not yearned for a cup of coffee on that fateful morning, realizing, of course, that he had a morning addiction.

Jocko Digby, CSA Vet of the Civil War, at 53 still with the keenest sniper's eye, counted the small list of gifts he could give to his lone daughter's wedding. Laura's mother would have done a better job than him, but lost herself inside a fire. Now it was necessary to create a gift, raise a gift, find a gift, make a gift ... but he was short on all points of that argument, down and out of silver, no dust in a locket-sized bag, "not even any coin for the tinklin'," as he shook a hand in an empty pocket.

"Have a beer," he said to himself, knowing it would not be so private, for he was known as an early celebrator, then muttered, "How to make something out of a flat nothing is the puzzle of the day, the puzzle of the year."

He'd not be able to make a puddle matter in the middle of a desert, his hands and mind lost in ineptness, that barren mind still talking to him as he looked out past the rim of the town, Duke Frazier's fence line running straight as a ruler across the wide grass, as though he owned everything in sight ... which he practically did.

"Get me latched into some kind of shootin' contest and I'll skunk the lot of 'em, the whole damned lot of 'em."

Laura's face that morning in the little cabin past the edge of town, and abutting Duke Frazier's large holding, was a sight to remember, a glow on her face the same way Molly'd greet each day regardless of what she knew was in store for her ... more work in Frazier's store, the man who owned, as was said of him, "He damned near owns every stick and stone and fence and rail and cow in the area. The man can damned well afford to lose a chunk of hisself if'n he had to, long as it was on the straight and narrow."

That phrase was about to stick in his mind.

Laura's smile, Jocko knew, was a cover-up, a pretense, for he figured she knew little if anything in the way of a present was to come her way this day. *There* was a guarantee somebody could bet on with a whole lot of certainty. "Winner take all!" He snuck a few looks at her, but never saw a giveaway, or a sign of it. Molly's daughter she was, every ounce and pound of her, every smile, every single smile through days which had turned out to be endless at times.

Those few words of his own spoken most immediately had backed him into his own corner. "Things *that* straight and narrow can't be let alone to be themselves. Got to be an edge for a gent like me, 'cause nobody in town's got a daughter like what Molly give me."

The internal argument began to find edges and reasons and rights for the cause. "I won't be able to lose. I can't lose. So I have to fix the odds my way." And he had lost his last horse in a card game that was probably fixed from the word go.

Jocko Digby switched his view down between two buildings and saw three poles of Frazier's fence line. They stood straight, tall and thick as beams and carried two beads of slim wire at this point, fitting Frazier's decree. "I'll have no thorny wire near the children of town. No barbed wire near the kids."

Jocko knew it had swung the whole town right into Frazier's camp. "Hook, line and sinker," he might have said if it had dawned on him.

But other ideas were on the flow in his mind, all leading up to his ability to buy Laura something for her birthday. "It's got to be quick. It's got to be clean. It's what I gotta win."

Then he thought again of the beer and empty pockets and Molly in the fire and him drunk somewhere in an alley.

There were a few odd things at the cabin he could sell, knowing some folks, especially some women folks, would buy anything from him, "Left alone with a beautiful daughter after that horrible fire."

He found a silver belt buckle, a mirror, a spoon with "maybe" some silver in it, and sold them to three ladies gathered outside the general store. The one thing he would not sell, besides Laura, was his rifle, a British-made, hexagonal-bored Whitworth with a telegraphic sight, and for him had provided power enough to drop targets at longer ranges than any other weapon he had tried in the war. This one he had brought home with him, home then being any place far to the west of long battle scenes against the Union army forces. He had knocked officers plumb off their horses under the most striking of conditions because of the smack and power of its ammunition, his eye as keen as any eye, celebrated he was as a sniper.

"Enough for a few beers for the day and some plannin'," he promised himself.

Walking toward the saloon, which happened not to belong to Frazier, he looked down between the two buildings at Frazier's fence line he had looked at earlier in the day, before the need for a beer sank in on him. His steps stopped, a single idea gripped him, and he was elated, a series of images, confrontations, up-front dares, and exceptional gambles to be undertaken.

A few actors he had seen in some traveling shows, and each one had learned his lines well, might well have the small drama completely memorized so that each could play any part in the usual three character dramas of such traveling shows. Each one was an expert in their own way, and their use of language, the tone of voice, their framed talk, lead audiences where they, the actors, wanted those audiences to go, lead them by the nose through plots think and thin.

It grabbed him again, the whole set of images, the imagined voices, the trickery of such voices, the false paths of audiences.

"Whither thou goest?" one of them once said on a stage set off by a length of canvas across three wagons lined up aside each other in a forgotten town on his way here, to this place, to this time. They spoke loudly, their voices crossing the town road, finding listeners on porches, on balconies, some even sitting horse-back, or holding a team of horses in the main road in order to hear the speakers and not intrude on the small and only occasional drama at hand.

He went to the saloon and as soon as he stepped in the door he heard Frazier say, "That gent was the best shot I ever saw." It must have been the end of a series of shooting stories.

The whole saloon was primed, including Frazier, thought Jocko, Then he said, "You ain't seen any shootin, yet. Like shootin' needles out of a gnat's eye."

Frazier laughed loud and long and finished by saying, "A toast to the Confederate sniper we all know about and screwing up the eye of a needle and a gnat's eye."

"Hell," Jocko replied, "I don't even know what a gnat is, but I can shoot the hell out of any man in here." He aimed along a pointed finger right at Frazier, who jumped out of shooting sight like an acrobat, still laughing at Jocko.

Jocko could feel the images begin to turn to the real thing. He walked to the door, looked down the main road to where the road turned to the right just before 7 or 8 visible poles of a Frazier fence line, cattle on the other side like an affront to the town itself.

Back to the bar he moved, spun about and said to Frazier, "I bet I could shoot down two of your fence wires right from the main road here near the saloon so they won't hold any cattle."

Everybody laughed, but loudest was Frazier.

Frazier, in turn, went to the saloon door and looked down the dusty road to where his fence line was struck across the edge of town.

He came back to the bar, looked all about, into sundry faces and sundry eyes and said, "You mean to tell me, even with your old sniper's rifle, you can shoot the two wires off my fence line so the cattle can't get through where those wires hold my cattle in place?"

"Yep, but only on a bet," responded Jocko.

Frazier, still laughing amid a joke of jokes, smiled anew and said, "What the hell you get to bet with, Jocko?"

"My little cabin and I'll even throw in my rifle I brought home from the war."

"What would have to be put up, my friend? What would someone like me have to wager on such a bet?"

"Oh, that'd be beyond anybody wantin' to bet, Duke. Don't you think?"

Frazier said, "Like what? Name it." His fist slammed down on the bar.

Jocko offered, "Only 100 cows, 100 acres to raise the cattle on, and a team of horses of my choice. I know that's too much for you, Duke. We can just forget it, if you want. Say it's done and over. Forget it. Say I'm a *Gone Goslin'*. I can take it."

"When?" Frazier was pushing.

"If I can borrow a horse, I'll go get my weapon. I've got it hid."

"By all means, my man, take my horse. Right out in front in his usual place." His smile was prairie-wide. Most saloon smiles were wide at that moment.

To a close observer, only the bartender was slowly shaking his head, but not fast enough to cause questions.

Jocko Digby was back in 20 minutes with his British-made, hexagonal-bored Whitworth sniper rifle with a telegraphic sight in place. To most observers he did not look a bit ferocious, or even really dangerous.

"Now let's get this straight," Frazier started to say, but Jocko cut him off.

"I'll kneel in the dust of the main street outside and with three rounds will disconnect the non-barbed wire in your fence so that your cattle can escape. Is that simple enough for you?"

Frazier, not at a loss for a wide grin, said, "It's your call, Mister Hawkeye."

The grin expanded.

The bartender slowly shook his head, but not one person in the saloon noticed the movement, as though, for the first time in this day, for many days, he was not there.

With a small bandolier of ammunition in place, Jocko Digby exited the saloon, moved into the dust of the road through the center of town. A pause caught at him and some thought he was about to back out of the deal. He looked down the street again, saw where the road turned to the right, saw the poles in Frazier's fence beyond the turn.

He also saw an image, a mile wide smile, a Molly smile, on the face of his daughter, as she stood watching him from the doorway of the general store.

He could not have been happier. He was glad he had not taken a drink. He heard the hush as the entire town went into an absolute silence.

With a very deliberate move, he loaded his weapon, brushed the telescopic sight with the tail of his dirty shirt as though it made no difference at all in the coming activities.

When he went to his knees in the dust of the main road even Duke Frazier had a moment's pity for him, but it did not last that full moment.

Others say it was near funereal, those moments, until the former Confederate sniper spun on his heel and knee and looked directly down alongside the saloon, where he had looked earlier at three fence poles of Duke Frazier's cattle fence, this group of poles at least three times closer than those at the end of town.

Duke Frazier, amazed by this turn of the event, was about to shout aloud, but Jocko Digby drew an eye on the middle pole of the three, squeezed off the trigger and saw the pole burst apart from the thunderous blast of the round tearing the pole in half, so that the upper half hung in the air, suspended by two wires connected to the other two poles.

Duke Frazier, aghast, looked at the bartender who looked back at him and offered a simple nod of his own.

The other two shots did as expected, two poles blown to bits by the thunderous shots and the opening in the fence line was as predicted by Jocko Digby who knew he was about to ride on a new kind of wagon and Laura'd have more presents than she could handle.

Molly finally had her way with things.

Bang! And the masked bandit fired from the saddle just as Harry Bantry reached down on the stagecoach boot to grab his rifle. The driver, Jim Foster, tasted Harry Bantry's blood as it spurted on his face; blood brothers forever was the first thought that hit him. A better brother he could not have chosen, but cold before he knew it. The only other memory of that sad day was the cry of the hawk as it rolled over on a thermal edge high above them, marking the place forever, that limitless and phantom space in the western sky. The sound stayed with Foster as if it was a monument of sorts, the cry as mournful as a late evening bugle call brought back from his 7th Cavalry days. He imagined the quivering lips of the bugler playing "Retreat."

If he ever did anything, it was to listen to himself think, which, even in hurry-up, was part of his long day, and much of his long nights.

Whenever he rode by the lone grave on top of Gladden Hill, the cross sitting pale in the morning light, he could see old Harry Bantry sitting beside him on the front seat of the stagecoach on the day it happened, his face full of the life that once bubbled in him. Three times now he had set a new cross in place, each time remembering with stark clarity how Bantry had taken the bullet that he believed was meant for him, the driver of the coach, the captain of the prairie schooner. The three years had fled like driven tumbleweed, bouncing along in jumps and spurts as if time could not be measured; him driving the stagecoach, Harry lingering around Gladden Hill until Kingdom come.

Not without all the echoes.

Each time it all came back with the sound of the shot, and then the faint, mysterious echo on the wind or the slightest breath of wind, half-heard, half-hidden, half understood:, Bantry saying, "Get 'im, Jim."

Leaving the station at Fairmont on this new morning, the temperature exactly like that memorable day, the shadows leaving the valley with the same speed as the sun crested every hilltop, he knew that other dawn as the station master said, "Three years ago this month, wornt it, Jimbo? Feels just like it, don't it, Jimbo?" like always answering his own questions. "If you was to remember, it was a day like this, wornt it? Can't you 'member that smiley face old Harry kept agrinnin' with, can't you? Like yesterday, wornt it, if you was to 'member it, eh, Jimbo?"

The newest shotgun rider, Josh Logan, only three rides under his belt, shook his head and said, "Man mutters a lot, don't he?" He looked back over his shoulder as they left the station proper, the thin curl of smoke rising from the little house on the flat meadow snuggled into the valley of Grogan Pass, Idaho's morning sitting flat on his face. "Mutterin's the least part of talk, I allus said."

Foster, for the three years since Harry had died, kept looking for something he had forgotten, something from that day; something besides the blood on his face, Harry getting cold in a hurry, the hawk turning over in the sky, how the wind touched his face that other morning when they set out.

All this time he knew there was a piece of information that he had known, had sensed, and had forgotten. No matter how many times he had tried, he could not bring it back. He could not see it, or smell it, or hear it. But it was there; of that he was sure. And Harry kept poking at him in one way or another to find it. "Get 'im, Jim," he had said. "Get 'im, Jim." It was like the day he was sworn into the army; duty was on him, all swift and powerful, enveloping him, to do whatever it was that it wanted him to do.

Oh, how he struggled again this morning, reaching, searching, hoping to find the elusive.

And he never knew it would be the insensitive new shotgun rider who would spring it up out of him, but it was all wondrous, how he sat mute at the reins, not hearing the shotgun talk or the horses' hooves beating their swift and staccato tattoo on the hard, dry ground of the road running for hours beside the half-green and half-stone mountain. And the coyote yelping out his wily dominion in a yet-shadowed valley where the sun hesitated in its visit and the darkness of night had not completely let go its hold, for peccaries ran apace and the wolves watched with practiced eyes, and deeper in the valley, in among the scattered upheaval and toss of rocks and trees bent over by the ages, an old Indian, almost old as time he believed, watched back down the trail for some white man to catch up to him and learn what he had learned long before they had come here, where the mountains rose to the moon and the prairie grass ran off to the mountains and the great waters and the tepee of Mahwahtopa himself, for he was to pass on the lessons of the hawk and the wolf and the coyote and the peccary, if only they would listen to him as they sat the proud mounts that leveled mountains and breasted formidable rivers and forced great herds to go where they wanted them to go into such deep maze-like defiles and wadis and gross canyons that they never came out again, not on this side and not on the other side, wherever that was where the growths came and taught you their names from the sides of the half-green mountains, like yucca and manzanita and agave and mesquite and pinon pine and juniper and arrow weed and bear grass and ocotillo and Douglas fir and ponderosa pine. All in such a music of names and uses and needs to be satisfied because the whole good Earth itself becomes the ultimate kettle and pot and pan and oven for sustenance, if they would stop to not only hear him but listen to him with a tuned ear, for their lives would so depend on what had already been learned by other men, up the wide paths from the Yucatan and down from the ice bridges in the north before the huge ships came from afar, from the places where thunder and lightning were issued and the very winds themselves.

Survival is knowledge, it all said to him, and bringing what you have known all the way along with you in journeys and travels wherever, as even he went now on this hard, dry road in view of those very same mountains, with the knowledge that was always his even though he now struggled to bring it all back from whence it had gone.

Something left over from that day he became Harry Bantry's blood brother.

The road came back to him, and the horses' hooves and the quiet sky spread like a camp blanket, and just as comfortable as he looked for a hawk, a crow, and then changed his squint to seek a dot in the sky, a verdin, a wren, something so insignificant he could forget it in a hurry, something that would take his mind onto another ride. He squeezed his eyes to a slit, and Logan was staring at him.

"What you looking at, Josh?"

"I'm lookin' tryin' to see what you're lookin' for. Must be hard to see nothin'. I don't see nothin' out there." He swung traversing his hand across the quiet sky, and slumped his shoulders to show he was perplexed. "Beats me to some kind of hollerin' if I let it."

He was a good looking kid and Foster liked him in spite of some shortcomings, which we all have he would have said if asked. The youngster's body language was straightforward. Foster acknowledged the fact by nodding his head at an angle, then he said, "I always have something on my mind besides the reins in my hands. Keeps the body in place, like riding and shooting at the same time, and you don't even realize one is different from the other."

In a second Foster was back looking at the road, listening to the hooves in their steady music as if drums were beating behind the horses or in the backs of their heads, the dust almost catching up to the coach moving swiftly on the dry bed of the road, the tension in the reins reading like a constant signal in his hands, knowing that the slightest yank might be understood by the lead horse shining in new sunlight that sat on his rump the way a chunk of broken glass catches sunrays in random fits. Knowing all the time he had heard something from young Logan that had not yet registered its meaning in his mind and he knew he was again at that point of departure when either his mind takes over his body fully or his body tells his mind to shut up and pay attention to the business at hand, which for that moment and that hour and that day was getting this coach to that point down the road and into one sweet valley where sweetness came in a big mug as clear as a spring waterfall off the face of a cliff. The knowledge of that sweetness came recovered in his throat the way he'd know a slice of peach at the end of a long day on the saddle and under the sun.

But young Logan was talking again. What had he said that had penetrated his mind, only to get lost in the mud he was sure at that moment was packed in there? He didn't think he had shut down his mind and had only let it slip by as unrecognized at the moment it was said. He thought about memory again, which brought him back to the smell of blood and the sound of the shot that Harry had caught in the worst place. He let a bit of slack slip onto the reins, let the lead black have a bit of temporary freedom, as if he could run away from the sound, the weight at his leathers no more than feathers in the driver's hands.

"Until you was to catch one in the belly, or in your shootin' arm. Saw a gent once, high in his saddle, catch a stray round and he fell like a rock off'n a porch roof." He looked at the sky again. Twisting his head, shielding his eyes with one hand even if he believed there was nothing out there, and continued. "You sure mix me up sometimes, Jim. I thought you was lookin' to see if you could see a hawk. I gotta tell you, I love to see them the way they roll over in the sky sometimes, free and easy as eatin' cooked beans at nightfall, like there's nothin' at all to it, just ride the wind like we ride them horses put in front of us, us leanin' on the whip or twistin' the reins on 'em."

"I like to see the hawks, too," Foster replied, "but they can be awful mean when they want to. Saw one grab a jack rabbit once and couldn't lift him up off the ground so he just about tore him in half so he could get a good portion back to the nest and the young ones. I stayed while he was gone about 15 minutes and he came back and took the rest in one more big chunk. One good hunter, that bird."

The hoof beats continued under them, the road continued ahead of them, the sky continued above them, and the mountain beside them, peaked with white wonder, taller than all that other silence in the world, continued alongside them as they rode along. Foster swore softly to himself, shaking his body in a rough manner, realizing that he could fall asleep in a second, could be hypnotized by his surroundings, the scene rolling by, the sound of the music filling the air, the hoof beats relentlessly synchronized, and him trying to beat up the dust in his mind where something was hidden from him.

Finally, as if he had snapped out of some memory complex, he heard Logan, his voice reverting almost back to his adolescent voice, say, "We was at a picnic once, tail end of a shivaree, and we were at the river, a whole bunch of us, and Linus Schroeber, a real joker kind of a guy, always good for a laugh, wore always a mustache stiffer than a brush and hair over his ears like it was a pelt, put a rabbit skin on his head and started dancin' around. Wham, a hawk came out of nowhere, sky or tree or cloud

I don't know where, and ripped those meat-hook talons at that skin and almost got old Linus in the neck area where the real blood is. Scared the hell out of all us." He shook his head, laughed a bit, and said, "Old Linus carries that scar right now, at least last time I saw him down river at Chatsville a few years back when they had the turkey shoot, and that scar runs clear across his ear and plumb onto his neck and lucky it didn't kill him one doc told him."

In one mad rush it all came back to Foster, that day the single shot spurted Harry Bantry's blood all over him, and the masked bandit, the killer shooter, turning sideways in the saddle and the scar on his neck becoming visible for that one second again, as it had before. And it spoke to him; knew he had seen that scar some place, on some man he had seen in a saloon, perhaps drinking right at the bar with him, tossing one down at the end of a dusty day and a dusty ride, the grit of sand in his clothes and on his hair stronger than dust, at a card table in a forgotten saloon trying to thumb the ace of spades just one countable time, at some way station on his coach route saddling a horse or leathering a mule, moving past him in the twilight coming down like mist outside the livery or, finally perhaps, stepping up on the fender into the darkness of the coach, into the dim part of his mind. The scar would be a good eight or nine inches long and might have killed another man, it looked so red and vicious. Foster remembered looking away so the man would not think he was staring at him, picking him for spectacle. Where was that? In what place he might have been a hundred times, or once, the day unknown, the season, the year? When Foster turned around the man had disappeared. He must have because he had never seen him again, but he was darn sure now that the scar on the killer was the same scar on the man who seemed to have moved out of his life. There could not be two of them, lest there were two stories of two men who had lived past two serious events. He'd not sum up the odds of that happening.

Young Logan, looking at the sky, searching out a hawk, really oblivious of what was happening around him, was talking a streak again, but Foster did not hear him, for now, at last, with an image fixed in his head, he could begin to look, could study every face he'd come across, at every stop and way station of his route along the Mogollons, beside the river, across the endless prairie with its endless trail, as the words kept riding on the air, "Get 'im, Jim. Get 'im, Jim."

The exacted promise, he knew, was fervent, was an oath.

And there'd be a new cross for Harry on the hill, next trip around.

Kennard Kenny Duques was the only sign of law for a hundred miles around the cow country of Hornbull, Texas, and Deacon Roger Delphin was the main source for the good word, where whispers made no intrusion. The pair had arrived there from opposite directions, little known about Duques and Delphin's background known as wide as a poster board; sought, hired away from a northerly town, and right to work from day one, burying cattleman Randell Dagos, mangled by a mad bull, marrying Claire Dumont and Chet Williams, blessing newborn Felix to Freighter Eddie Calhoun's wife, Bobby-Joe Calhoun.

Duques was a different story ... or rather, no long story but a quick exposé. A stranger to the bartender at the Hornbull Saloon, to all of all the men that fateful day when one other stranger shot and killed a man in a card game. Duques had seen the killer playing a second game with an ace up his sleeve, dared to call the point out to all those in the saloon, and drew his own gun when the cheater went for his weapon. Duques' speed was spotlighted by all in attendance.

When a proposal was put forth by the saloon owner, Jack Reynolds, that Hornbull needed a sheriff, Duques was hired ... for that one shot. He didn't fire his pistol for three months, not until the day he heard a shot and checked out the minister's house at the very edge of town, and found him dead of a wound in the back of the neck, as if an execution had taken place.

There was hell to pay, and town folks stood around waiting to be formed up as a posse, venting their anger, showing the loss vividly, waiting to make amends.

Making his way out of the milling crowd, Duques moved around the edges of town, talking to anybody he met, knocked on a few doors, even stopping to talk to some of the children he came across.

One child, of about seven or eight, pleased to be spoken to by the new sheriff, admitted he had seen a stranger on a black horse riding as if he was headed out of town. "Was pointed to Turkey Hill where my uncle Joe lives. My Pa goes there sometimes but I've never been there. It seems so far away. He's gone for two days."

"What kind of horse was he riding? Are you Joe Thornton's nephew, him from Turkey Hill? I know him. What kind of a horse was the man riding?"

"A big black. I mean a big one. And he wore a dirty hat." He was anxious to stress that point.

Duques said, "Who, the man or the horse?" The two laughed in unison and the boy slapped his thigh just the way Duques had seen his father do it, with gusto and showmanship.

"Nah, not the horse, Sheriff," he corrected in a falsely-understandable manner, "the man riding the horse. He wore a dirty gray hat the kind my mother would scream if my father hung it on the rack by the door. Says the house is her holy place and it's going to stay that way." He smiled up at the sheriff and added, "She only says it about a hundred times a day," He held his hands far apart in measurement.

The two again laughed in unison.

In the morning, two hours before noon, a big man wearing a dirty gray hat and riding a big black horse, came riding into town as if he had ridden from Mosquito Junction, another two day's ride which is the other way from Turkey Hill. Duques had never seen him before ... but knew enough about him to warn himself of possibilities, life's dangers, things once done are done easier the next time around, a shooter's apprehensions.

What he did surmise was the man did not leave Mosquito Junction on this day, might have ridden around Hornbull, and stayed the night out of sight, to prepare his ride into town this day, falsify his whereabouts, his starting point of travel, hiding some issues.

Duques believed he had his first suspect in the execution of Deacon Roger Delphin. All he had to do was sit by, keep the man under observation, make him itchy as all get-out.

He started his watch at the saloon, shooing well-wishers out of the line of vision with a bit of trickery or small white lies about what he was up to, as though it was a day off work for him. Cagily he locked up data on the man: his table and drinking mannerisms, what he favored in liquor, how he treated the lone waitress, how he signaled her or the bartender when he was ready for another round, how often he looked around the room for anybody too curious, ever alert to how and where Norman wore his two pistols in holsters an Indian might have decorated (a fact little Joey Thornton hadn't mentioned), how he shifted in any slight discomfort where his weapons seemed crunched or crowded, not set for a quick draw.

The suspect's name was, supposedly, Gregg Norman, and there was not a single note about him at the sheriff's new office among the *wanted collection*. More than once, with his eyes screened, he managed to see Norman turn and look at him. No direct eye contact was made, but it was obvious to Duques that the suspect Norman was getting nervous.

The situation become a little touchy when the owner Reynolds sat at Duques' table blocking the line of sight to Norman. "I've been watching you, Sheriff, what the Hell are you up to, staring across the room?"

Norman didn't jump up at Reynolds' loud observation, but leaned forward, as if to disappear into the table top or merge with his table companions.

"Just relaxing for an hour or so," Duques responded.

"What from?" Reynolds said, "You ain't fired that gun of yours since you got appointed as sheriff. Must feel strange on your hip." He slapped the table to wake up the whole saloon and continued, "That one shot you took might have run all around the territory. Gone off there ahead of you, a favor done. Maybe nobody wants anything to do with you, including the rat who shot the deacon in the back of the neck like the rat he is. That must be the lining on the cake for you, sitting still the whole of an afternoon in my saloon who dragged the vote all for you. Mighty nice work if you can get it as they say back in Beantown where I come from. Mighty nice work."

Duques hoped the loudmouth was done when he stood up and said to all listeners, "Don't go against any of the law, you gents, 'cause the sheriff has the whole day off."

Reynolds only took two steps, jerked his head sideways and said, "I heard you were talking to the Thornton kid about some rider on a big black horse. Did that take you anywhere on your day off? Any leads? Hell, there's a big black outside right now tied at the rail. That lead you anyplace, Sheriff?"

Duques wanted scream at Reynolds, but whispered, "Keep your mouth shut about the kid, or I'll shut it for you." The Death Sign was already hanging around the boys neck.

"You work for me, Sheriff, in case you don't know it. I got you your job, me. I got it. You wear your badge and don't tell me what to do. Did you even check out who rides the big black? I bet you didn't sitting here, resting from nothing. Haven't even fired one shot since you took the job."

Norman stood beside his table, twin guns hanging in their holsters an Indian surely decorated, the afternoon sun making the fancy trim sparkle, all eyes attentive to the classy workmanship. "That's my horse, Reynolds. I came in from Mosquito Junction earlier this morning. What's it to you?"

A sense of belligerency passed through the room as though fire was going to come among all the customers. Some men, veterans of wars forgotten for a time, were afraid to breathe, afraid to be marked again, afraid to see friends go down for the final time.

At that moment, at the moment of memory and threat combined, the young Thornton lad raced into the room yelling at the top of his voice, "Hey, Sheriff, that horse I told you about, the big black one, he's the one outside right now tied at the rail. I know it's him."

The boy's eyes went from Sheriff Duques to Reynolds and then to Norman standing beside his table, where his eyes spotted the decorated holsters on Norman's belt, the sun coursing through the windows lighting the edges like a silver lode.

The scream was loud, his fingers pointing to Norman. "That's him. Sheriff, those are the same holsters he was wearing yesterday. I know that for sure. The same ones from yesterday."

Norman went for his guns.

Duques was quicker. Surer. Not a round wasted onto the side wall of the saloon where Norman's slugs went in the deadly duel between two souls.

Reynolds had grabbed the boy and drove him to the floor with him, out of harm's way. Other customers had scattered to floor or to recesses behind furniture, walls, semi-darkness, most remembering duels and firefights they'd been in or witness to, silence once again playing its sudden part.

Norman stood, mouth ajar, yet unable to say the holiest or even the foulest of words, whatever he went searching for, still wondering why he'd been paid to kill a man of the cloth, not that it made any difference any longer in this short lifetime.

Sheriff Kenny Duques, unique gunsmith, deadly shooter, assured of the safety of the Thornton boy, headed off to Mosquito Junction the following morning.

He was never seen in Hornbull, Texas again.

Deacon Allie Jones studied a crude map of Texas he'd found on the trail near a campsite long since used, the ashes in the ring of stones blown with the wind, and the ring disturbed by man or beast. He accepted the discovery as a sign sent to him. Without thought, he reached and patted a shaggy-looking dog by his side. "Good boy, Duke," he said, "and He still attends."

Plum dead in the center of the crude map, blazoned with a dark circle of black pigment of unknown source, was the name of *Willstock*, as though it was sent to him as a directive from straight overhead. Images of the unseen community rushed into his mind. He apprehended a scattering of small cabins and houses, a store with supplies piled on its front porch, a jail made of rock and tree parts and a few iron bars making it appear to be the strongest structure in Willstock.

His mind quickly made up, a journey already in place in his thoughts, he attended as usual the campsite another person had organized, setting stones back in order of use, piling loose logs close at hand to the fire pit, leaving a container, too big to lug on his horse, full of water from the nearby stream. It was Providence directing his care and comfort for the lost, the lonely, the forlorn who might pass this way, as he had, and found divine direction.

The good feeling, he knew, would stay with him until the journey brought him all the way to Willstock, in the heart of Texas, perhaps two days ride for him and for Lucky Lu, his horse and for the shaggy dog.

The sun at a low angle, evening descending to sleep, he saw on the surface of the water-filled container, his face looking back at him. He'd shaved the edges a bit, left his dark mustache and beard in place, trimmed his thick eyebrows and the few hairs protruding from his nostrils. That nose had been broken only once, in his early years, and widened little in his forty years. With a heavily accented cough of approbation, he accepted his appearance for the moment, not at all thinking what the ride would do to him, checked Lucky Lu one last time, spread his blanket and fell half asleep, an edge of alertness in tow, shaggy Duke near at hand.

In the morning, before he left this site, he'd take care of Lucky Lu and Duke, make a cup of coffee, eat some crackers or dip hard bread into his coffee, several such meals planned en route for him.

The trail might swallow him at times, but he'd get to Willstock; he'd been sent there by special means.

In mid-morning of the third day, he entered Willstock to see a small crowd mingling in front of the obvious general store, a man in a black robe sitting at an impromptu desk, gavel in his hand, saying aloud, "Nate Slack, you've been a bully for your whole life, a foul-mouthed beast, a tormentor of our women and children, a man very few can call friend, you are going to hanged by your rotten neck until death takes you, as this court has found you guilty on all accounts of which I speak, not just the fiendish murder of Harold Martin, once beloved of all of us."

A burly, robust man, tied with heavy rope with heavier-looking knots, astride a horse, said, "He was a rat in a man's skin, all of us know that if you'd think about it. But I didn't kill him. I keep telling you I didn't kill him. I'd spur this horse into a run if I did. I may be a lot of things, but I am not a coward. I don't kill men from behind, from darkness, from cover, from cowardice. That's shooting a fish in a barrel, and not my style."

The robed man said, "We all know it could only be you who did this foul deed, this fiendish execution of a respected man, and we're going to make you pay for it."

"You won't get any money from me on this account, not a penny; I didn't do it. Not a soul has stood up in this stupid session and said they saw me do it. Not one of you. Because none of you can say it and be the truth from the one God all of you swear by or to or for, whatever swings in your souls."

Nate Slack, the rope already around his neck, looked around at familiar faces in the crowd, saw how each one hesitated to look back into his eyes, looked instead at their own feet standing in the middle of the dusty road. "Who'll say he thinks I might not have done it?"

"Whoa," said the robed man, "Don't try to manipulate the crowd. The verdict is in. Only you could have done it and we all know it."

Slack said, "Now you're trying to get them to stay on your side, so I'll swing by the neck here in front of all of you, stock sure I did it, and feel okay about it as a crowd of one. That's what you are, a crowd of one. Where are the men among you? Why did I always pick on you? None of you will fight me back, never stood up to me, but one of you, the real coward of Willstock, stands in front of all of us, in among us, and might do it again to anybody who speaks about this in the future."

Not a murmur came from the gathering, the assigned judge with the gavel still raised on high, when Deacon Allie Jones nudged Lucky Lu forward through the crowd and grasped the reins of the horse Slack sat upon. The dog stayed in place at the edge of the crowd.

"Hold it, Your Honor, Your Judgeship, whatever you can call yourself, this whole thing sounds like a travesty on the heart of justice."

The reins of the second horse were tight in one of the Deacon's hands, the other was too close to one of his holstered weapons, too close to spur any defiance.

"Who are you, Sir?" said the robed one, leaning forward in his seat. "You're not one of us."

"You are right on that account, Sir," Deacon Jones said, "I am not one of you. I'd be ashamed to be one of you."

"The who are you that you can bust in on this court?"

"This is not a court, Sir. This is a travesty about to happen. I am Deacon Allie Jones sent here by the Good Lord, He on the Most High, to do the right thing for this man accused of a crime that not one soul among you saw and spoke that mind. A travesty on this crowd, on all of Willstock from this day forward if it is allowed to happen."

A nervous rustling, interpreted as doubt by the Deacon, started at the edge of the crowd, those farthest from the presiding judge, but that rustling, as if a spirit was found in it to gather strength, moved through those townsmen collected to see the death of one of their own.

"What church do you represent, Sir? We have no church here, I'll have you know. How can we accept you?"

"You will have a church, Sir, whether it's just a temporary tent I will put up, or we adopt one of these structures to house its beginning, like this store perhaps that's been adopted by the court."

"This is my store, Sir. I own it. I allow it to be a court when necessary."

"Then you'll have no objection to it housing a church, even temporary in nature, and a court as well, as we would prepare and present a new defense for this man so unjustly accused of murder without witness."

The Deacon held tightly the reins from the possible death horse. "If you agree to what I propose, I'd like to see this man untied and dismounted before a shot goes off and messes up this town forever."

The store owner-judge, backed down by a stranger, casually waved his hand, and Nate Slack was freed of ropes and the noose around his neck, and dismounted on his own.

"Thank you, Sir," the Deacon said, and asked, "What is your name, Sir?"

"I am Gregory Buckman, storekeeper, store owner, judge, and now housing what church?" The previous humor in his face had disappeared.

"The church of the One God, the Church of Him who sent me here, with such information to be presented to you at an early convenience, which would be after a meal for me and this man who so recently had the noose of death around his neck. I am sure he'd like to share a meal with me."

"I'll buy," said the judge, tearing off the black robe without his previous dignity.

The three men ate a meal at a corner table of the saloon when Deacon Jones said, "And you, Mr. Buckman, do not own this place too? Is there a reason for this?"

"I sell goods, so I'm a storeowner. I am a teetotaler, so I don't own a saloon."

"But you work at being a judge but you don't deal in justice. That affair earlier was as close to travesty as I've seen. Why is that?"

"I'd guess it's my assumption I could be a judge in these matters, but realize what you told me to be true. I'm not a dispenser of justice. I was sure from what I heard about Mr. Slack here, that he was guilty, the only one who could be guilty of the crime. The whole town seemed to feel that way."

"That's why Willstock needs a man of the cloth, to steer them away from such apathy, death followed by another needless death, haste of waste, need of deed, din of sin."

Buckman was nodding assent as if thoughts had come into his mind, and Nate Slack sat open-mouthed for the first time in a long time, and Deacon Allie Jones slapped one of his holstered pistols and remarked, "Those are reasons I have not fired a shot in months."

At that very instant, as if punctuation for his statement, a shot went off outside, a woman screamed, "Somebody shot my husband." She screamed a second time.

Deacon Jones rushed to the door of the saloon, and yelled out, "Shooter, Duke. Shooter, Duke."

Duke, in a sudden leap at the command, ran directly to the outermost building in Willstock, a dwelling on the second floor and a leather shop on the first floor. As if practiced in other searches, Duke looped once around the building and stood out in front of it, firm-legged, head up, barking at the upper floor.

It was, as it appears, cut and dried, finding a man with a smoky rifle hiding in a closet space, a man known as an excellent shot on hunting forays.

Buckman, more alert than ever, open-minded at the proliferation of evidence, sought out his discarded robe and set about to convene court once more. This time he had witnesses ... of a sort ... and knew a comfort in his work. He was already designing a church in his mind.

When beloved Welcome "Kucky" Ross was shot by a bushwhacker, no range war rampant, nor enemies of common knowledge, two of Texas' cattle barons met at the boundary of their ranges after interment, to discuss the death of a son, a son-in-law as well.

Both men were heart-broken and neither one tried to hide his feelings, though they had long been on opposite sides of many deals. "He's my son, too," his father-in-law said, the words drawing the two men tighter than they might ever have been.

Welcome Ross, I, had carved out his ranch on the wide grass with years of effort, the ranch known as The Duke's Edge. Father-in-law Jade George, Junior, of the Bull's Head, had inherited his property from his mother, who died only two months after her husband, from a bushwhacker's bullet also, a quickly dispatched posse only finding a horse trail faded into a wind storm that forced the retreat of the posse, their return to home, no guilty party named, no resolution ever determined.

Sadness and loss had brought these ranchers closer.

The latest victim, 24 years old, was born as Welcome Ross, II, on a celebrated day for grandparents owning two of the largest ranches in Texas, to the daughter of one of those ranches, and her husband from the other ranch. There was a huge celebration at his birth, a boy welcomed and so named for his arrival by parents and grandparents. A few folks said he was born laughing, "or at least smiling through the whole ordeal."

It was evident he had a head start on the good life for those times in the wide stretches of Texas.

The burial was put off for days to allow the word to spread, which brought visits from every hand who had once worked for either ranch in Kucky's time.

It quickly became known that two younger siblings had nicknamed Welcome, II, as Kucky, whatever way it might be spelled, from a day when he soiled his pants riding an untamed pony wild as a pig with a poke.

With that nickname, obviously on for the long ride, he developed a remarkable sense of humor, treating the name as if given to him by the Overhead, amusement abounding in him at its use, accepting the taunts and harsh words thrown as taglines to the name. With duty, acceptance, non-interruption, he responded to the name immediately. It set him for all to see, as friendly, affable, but serious of name calling. No other name came in the calling.

Priscilla George, Prissy to one and all, never once addressed Welcome, II, as Kucky; from an early age she had decided he was the man she'd marry one day ... and he'd not be Kucky to her. Her father spoke his negative thoughts until he observed his dead wife, and Prissy's mother, coming back in his daughter, and wisely backed down. He'd been caught in that twist before.

Prissy, of a certainty, handled the proposal: "You will marry me before I turn 22 or never. That's all I'll say, and if you agree, we can seal our love this very night." The stunning went both ways, as she received more than what she dreamed. They were together, she thought, forever, until the world fell down on top of her.

She had proposed, loved, married, was bearing a child ... and widowed, in that first year.

She told her father and father-in-law, "You get him, who took my husband, or I swear I'll go looking myself, before his child is born."

The two men met at the range line on a splendid day, but crowded by loss and threats and dire promises of the expectant mother of Kucky Ross's child.

In the employ of both her father and father-in-law she had a few close friends among the ranch hands, especially those that had hung with her husband in his early years and/or worked trail with him in good times and hard times. She selected hard riders, tough workers, good listeners, smart interpreters of innuendo, rumor, campfire talk, bar talk sober or drunk they might hear concerning the father of her unborn child.

Four men she commissioned for the tasks explained to them as a group at a very secretive meeting, swearing each one to secrecy, loyalty and dogged search for the simplest of clues, remarks accidentally exploited, slurred at bar or poker table, or in raucous story telling at trail camps and similar gatherings ... daring to call them Kucky's Rangers, or the KR Boys.

She'd send them in a variety of directions, to nearby towns and villages, across the state of Texas, and into some of those places bordering Texas including the Mexican States of Chihuahua, Coahuila, Nuevo León, and Tamaulipas to the southwest, and U. S. states of Louisiana to the east, Arkansas to the northeast, Oklahoma to the north, and New Mexico to the west. If necessary, the waters of the Gulf of Mexico would be targeted.

"That," she said to herself in sound concern, "will be enough to set them to work from the first word."

They responded with sworn determination to unearth the Earth itself to find the thinnest leads concerning the death of their friend.

One of them, from her father's ranch, was a rugged and handsome cowboy, veteran of four drives north. Steve Anchor was the quietest of the lot, stared deepest into her eyes at explanations and reasons, and the only one who asked by what means they might relay information to her if it could not be brought directly to her person.

She reacted womanly, with quickness, bright ideas, and a side-saddle of humor. "Pretend, in any manner you wish, that you are seeking my favor. You may not realize the payment, but it will ease the burden on all of us to get Kucky's killer."

It was the first time any of them had heard the name from her.

As she might have foretold, it was Steve Anchor who reported back first, a note to her delivered by messenger, simply saying, "The best prospect for a new sheriff, mouthy on the cause carries a new Sharps in his saddle, the long range beauty now for sale. He drinks rum. Always has a cigar lit, smokes 'em to the stub. Worked short time *TDETH*, will revisit this fined village twene ArborsV LudlumT cigar fire rumble."

Prissy smiled at her interpretation, Anchors' language concepts, resigned to its meaning, "I have met a man who spoke ill of your Kname, carries a new long-range Sharps in his saddle sheath, smokes cigars to the final stub, once worked for a time at The Duke's Edge, TH his initials, in a saloon between Arborsville and Ludlumtown drinking rum. I will track him down again in towns named."

TH, in a quick session with one older foreman, was revealed as a cowpoke named Thorn Hurley who was let go for lack of effort.

She called in another trusty soul, Martin Reed, young, imaginative, one of her favorites, and said, "Draw a map with a circle around it where my husband was killed, Marty. The size of the circle should be determined by the distance a long range newer Sparks rifle would be effective. Mark all the spots you find where a man could hide and with a clear sighting shoot and kill Welcome. I hear those new Sharps rifles are excellent weapons. Don't mark any spot where sight is obstructed by a rise in the ground, trees, boulders, a shack or barn or a lean-to. It has to be a clear view. Be particular about any place you find with cover behind the shooter, keeping him out of general sight. It's a hard job, takes some decisions, but I know I can trust you all the way, Marty."

A look went across Prissy's face as though a moment of unseen history was playing itself out. Then her look changed and she said, "You know what I mean, a place where a killer, a back-shooter'd pick out just like I've explained to you. I know it's spooky business, but maybe you can do what he did in setting up Welcome as a target. Mark them all, the good spots. I'm going searching when you're done. It's wild stuff, but it could be the very first lead that's to come out of all of this."

Her hand touched his arm. "Don't tell my father or Welcome's father, Marty. Do it as a favor for me. I want the killer caught before this baby's born." She patted her swelling full of coming life. "There's a bonus in it for a good job." Her expression could have swept up the whole world for her.

"Yes, Ma'am," he gulped, to a woman younger than he was, even as she wondered who'd get back to her first, Marty Reed or Steve Anchor. Both of them, before the other two searchers, would be out and about where she wanted to be in the limited amount of time she had to work on her end of a murder demanding to be solved.

It was almost with a divine hand in the matter when Marty Reed showed her his map, with a dozen possible places where a shot could be fired.

But one mark was bolder than the others.

"This place here, by that small crop of rock and boulders sticking out of the ground like it came from the middle of the earth in the middle of the night, and trees behind it. Even a horse would be out of sight there. It's the perfect place."

An embarrassing smile fixed his face, an apologetic smile, an innocent-as-all-Hell smile.

Prissy smiled, touched by his innocence, his youth, and said, "I know the place. Let's ride out there. You see any shell casings around?"

"Not a thing," he replied, "and I did look around. Old tracks was all I saw, dozens of them, range riders out of the sun, maybe for a rest, slop his hat for water for his horse." He shrugged, as though his mission had been diminished in its intent.

Prissy Ross searched the ground from one part of morning shade to the end of it, the rock as craggy as any ill-formed cluster thrust up out of the ground a thousand or more years earlier. She was on her hands and knees much of the time, scratching away at dirt, running her fingers through it, now and then resting as if the new weight she carried was talking to her, telling her to rest.

"You oughten't be down there like that, Prissy. It's not good for you. And I did what exactly you're doing now ... and found nothing. Not a sliver of a thing. Nothing." He put his hand out to help her get up from the ground.

She rose slowly, thanked him, and then began scouring on the rock formation as if lightning had hit it a dozen times, rending and chipping it, making cracks and fissures in the faces of the element.

And there! In one crack! In one horizontal fissure, the first solid clue! One she had been looking for. Retrieving something from that crevice, she slipped it into her shirt pocket. "Let's go, Marty, I'll never be able to thank you enough. She hugged him.

They rode back to the ranch. Once in a while Marty Reed saw her hand feeling the mound on her stomach, making him extremely nervous.

But determination, dedication, effort, and thorough work often come together for erstwhile souls, for as they approached the ranch house they saw Steve Anchor riding toward them from further west, waving his hat in the air.

"I found him, Prissy. He's been seen in The Cross Trails Saloon in Ludlumtown, only a few hours' ride from here."

At her direction, the two hands mustered a crew of six more men, each one newer at the ranch, and all set out for the short ride, a posse commissioned en route.

Steve Anchor checked out the saloon, came back and said, "He's in there, playing cards, cigar lit up. Not too many folk there yet."

Prissy sent in three men ahead of the others, telling them to be noisy and regular on entrance, and go right to the bar as they usually would.

When she walked in with Marty Reed and Steve Anchor she put a gun to the back of Thorn Hurley's neck. She jabbed it tightly against his neck as she felt a labor pain strike through her body.

"Thorn Hurley, we're arresting you for the bushwhacking murder of my husband, Welcome Kucky Ross." She slipped her free hand into her shirt pocket, withdrew it, and dropped the stub of the cigar butt onto the tabletop in front of Thorn Hurley, the stub she'd found stuck in the crevice of the bushwhacker's shooting spot.

Steve Anchor disarmed Hurley, and Marty Reed grasped Prissy Ross as her labor pains suddenly intensified.

Welcome Kucky Ross, III, was born in The Cross Trails Saloon in Ludlumtown, Texas on the 28th day of August in 1879. He lived until the ripe old age of 88, at the Duke's Edge Ranch, where he is buried in a family plot. He lies beside his mother, father, grandfather, grandmother, and a number of ranch hands alone in their world.

Broccin Mac Dubbacin was his given name, all its historic way from 12th century Gaelic Scotland, every hoot and holler of it, until his father brought him and a sister, and his wife, across the Mississippi River in a move from Scottish hills afire with torments to a section of Kansas, called Baxter Springs. It was sometime before the war of the states, the boy then a robust 13-years old. In short order, in saloon odds and ends and stories galore, he was introduced, this boy at his father's side come hell or high water or trouble of any sort, as Bronco Dubbins. His name spilled from his father's mouth at the first card game at a saloon table in a newer town in the territory, also looking for a proper name and found it as Baxter Springs.

So named is our hero and our locale.

At that moment the small town in the lower part of Cherokee County was called Baxter Springs, a small but somewhat friendly and calm chunk of the Kansas Territory before it was organized as a state later on, in 1861. The year of their arrival was in the 1850's, and torment still looking to be the family inheritance.

Big Mac, as his father was called by the locals ("them sho'ders a his're big as plow horses,"), was handed a sheriff's star practically at arrival, at least after his first round of stories about his homeland caught up in its own fire, like much of that running around Baxter Springs, and it needing a man like Big Mac right smack in the middle of things. He appeared to be the needed type, a family man looking for the better life, and guaranteed to protect what was his family and his new piece of property, "won by gosh in a wild poker game endin' in hurried dispute and quick death of the loser whose inside straight, all them cards red too, was not good enough to keep his property, and made him draw on the Scot and die at his hand."

Some men, in this new part of the new world, are brought to fame's door by the simplest actions of a good draw at either the cards or the pistol spouted at the hip. Such men, as it happens, often as not, also bring their sons on their fabled journeys, exampled as here presented.

That rough and tumble Gaelic warrior, Big Mac survived nearly 20 years of service to the small community as it grew into its surrounding shadows, the low hills, the cattle-favoring land, as his son, the aforementioned Bronco Dubbins, grew with him. The community, was the same kind of being as his father, but fiercer on wild horses needing training and keener and deadlier with pistol and rifle.

Those early toys became tools in his hands.

As war progressed, came within earshot of the small Kansas town, the Fort Baxter Massacre took place in 1863, and the boy, Bronco

Dubbins, then a galvanized hunk of man on foot or horse, knew how the oats worked him, even as he was heading toward home. He heard the shooting coming from the fort under fire from Southern sympathizers under the leadership of outlaw William Quantrill, not more than a kid in his own right.

It was there that a young lieutenant, James Burton Pond, from his actions, was awarded a Medal of Honor in the on-going battle against an element of Quantrill's Raiders, but his senior officer was captured and was being tortured roadside by the raiders when the then 18-year old Dubbins rode his fire-eating stallion into the midst of the raiders torturing the captured officer, whose screams had raised the skin of those within hearing distance.

Those hearing the screams included young Dubbins.

Heedless of his own safety, it was said immediately thereafter, he rode his stallion, black as Hell itself, perhaps an original version of a Jayhawker, into the midst of Quantrill's men, pistols in hand, hooves of his mount slashing away at command, driving off the overpowering unit, until he was able to hustle the officer onto his stallion and brought him to safety.

To the country, only Lt. Pond was so highly treated, and written about, but locals began to tell the real story of Bronco Dubbins, so that it began its own history, having its own patronage when locals gathered in later years, just as they did for long months after the war was over. New shadows came calling.

Heroes, of a certain, have their own foes, enemies, doubters, in all walks of life, love and battle. So, Bronco Dubbins, later wearing the star his father wore for those 20 years of service until shot from behind by an unknown sniper, no follow-up boasting, murmurs or whispers, no stable or bar talk, for the ensuing quiet years after the war had ruptured the land.

That was so, until a nocturnal visit was made to a grave, plainly marked for a Scot's grave, as Broccin Mac Dubbacin, Sheriff. The grave was on the land once owned by Dubbacin, then by his son, Bronco Dubbins, who sold it to a young couple, Joseph and Miriam Phersain. Joseph brought to Bronco a note left at the gravesite: "Near the 20th year when I put this man down from near 100 yards."

Wild and wooly Bronco Dubbins, Sheriff, for his own 20 years, did not scream or swear vengeance as perhaps he might have wanted, but sat in his office chair a whole week at thought. Never once did he venture to the saloon, the barbershop, the general store, to inquire if any new faces with old names had recently been seen in town, nor ask if a lost face had been seen one single time since his father's murder, or a cowpoke who came back to collect a debt or some pay owed him.

Not one question from him for three days.

For three days he sat inert, some saying sadness finally had a grip on him.

Then, as if waking from a sordid dream, escaping old memories, he asked everybody concerned or apt to know, the names of those people once of Baxter Springs and the local area whom they had not seen in 20 years. There were not many takers, but some folks with good memories advanced their lists, and the combined lists were drawn into one non-repeating list of 33 names of men not seen thereabouts for about 20 years.

He went to see the mayor of Baxter Springs, Knute Fellows, a kindly sort, a twinkle in his eye, who once a month would walk into the saloon and grant a free drink to all at the bar. Some folks, seeing him enter would scramble for the bar and he'd make note of them, all in a joking manner.

"What can I do for you, Bronco? You have a set look on your face."

Bronco told him what he had done, what was in his mind, how the mayor could help him. "Just spread the word, Mayor, that I'm seeking out these men on this list. Sooner or later, wherever they are, and I'll track down every one of them, when they see me coming towards them, down a main street, across a trail campground, on a cattle drive anywhere, they'll know what I'm up to, to hang the man who killed my father, long-range, like a coward, and they let me know one way or another if they are the guilty party."

"By gosh, Bronco, I don't know another man who could have put that together like you did. It's priceless. I'd love to be there when the guilty party goes for his gun. But I'll do as you ask with one favor: Don't shoot to kill him but wound him and bring him back for his hanging. That's all I ask."

"That's fine with me, Mayor, and you can appoint my deputy as sheriff because I'm starting my journey this day."

Bronco Dubbins was out of the trail before nightfall working his way across three state borders, into dozens of towns and ranch sites out again, meeting up with many old faces. Some of them had heard about his search, and some had not; some greeted him as an old friend or acquaintance, some spoke well of his father, some expressed their sorrow at his loss and at his necessary errand.

One man said, "I know it's hard losing your father, I lost mine in a bank robbery. He was a teller at the bank and they got the man who shot him dead, but it's sure a long journey you might be facing. I wish you luck and him whoever all the bad luck you've got in your saddlebag."

Thirteen names on the list had been tracked down and faced, and none of them appeared to be the deadly sniper, as Bronco was convinced in each case, some admittedly after a hard study in nervous cases.

One cowpoke, now a foreman on a large spread way up on the cattle drive trail, admitted his long-held secret. "I always had suspicions about a couple of gents, whose names you may not want on your list, which a few folks have told me about. I think, if I was you, you'd rather not hear any names from me but get him just the way my cousin, Knute Fellows, advised me, almost said it word for word like I did. You sure made him sit up and take notice, and he has spread the word far beyond Kansas I'll bet, up to the lakes and all down the big rivers. You really put this thing together after a lot of thought, didn't you? Knute thinks it's brilliant, but sure is calling for lots of time and travel on your part. Want to light here for a few days? No problem at all with the big boss 'cause we already had a talk about you. We knew you were comin' this way."

He added, "That's the big kick in all this, ain't it? Scarin' the hell out of somebody from as far away as you might be right now. Powerful stuff, Bronco. Pure powerful."

He patted the lone searcher on the back in the manner of a salute well-earned.

Bronco had checked off 18 names, the first crack appearing in his own drive for justice, a middling kind of feeling he had for the first time, and was approaching Ellsworth, Kansas, after being in such places as Caldwell, Wichita, Newton and Abilene, much of the time on or just off the cattle drive trails on the routes north.

But always a name to check, a face to look at, eyes to look behind.

He dismounted at the outskirts, in front of the stable, and said to a young stable hand, "Treat him well, son. He's been a great mount for me. His name's Purple, and I'm looking for an old acquaintance name of Crate Smithers. You know him?"

"Heck, yes, mister. Old Crate himself just left here a few minutes ago and we was atalkin' an' ajawin' a whole hour 'bout practicly nothin', way he is."

He looked up the street, about halfway along a group of odd buildings, and pointed out a man just about to mount his horse in front of the saloon, and yelled, "Hey, Crate, an old pard's here lookin' for you." He pointed at Bronco, near big as his horse about to be tied-off at the stable rail.

The man up the street jumped up on his horse without using the stirrups and headed, quicker than a rabbit runs, down the dusty road, out of town at a high gallop.

Bronco yelled at the young stable hand, "Better go get the sheriff, son, Tell him I'm a sheriff myself, after a wanted killer, and I'll bring him back after I catch up with 'im. Have a doc handy too when we come back."

In a likened action, quick as he'd ever moved, Bronco Dubbins was in his saddle and in flight.

The trio of horsemen, three abreast, were just about to enter midnight's lonely road of Broken Hill, Texas, when a slug of a rifle shot hit the dust ahead of them.

The shot, obviously, was a warning, and the middle rider held up his hand and loudly said, "We're here looking for work. We heard this town is going to be rousted again and we want to offer our help. We're not useless in these situations. Never have been and we been in a few tight spots over the years, Texas itself being our home."

A voice from the dark said, "Who are you? Identify yourselves. Where you coming from?" Gentle rustling sounds came from various places along the road, from some rooftops but no one showed themselves. The silence came again after the few words, the speaker not yet seen, hidden on some rooftop, around a corner perhaps.

The middle rider, moving around on his saddle, fully exposing himself to a possible second shot, said in a thick voice, a mix of Texas and wide elsewhere in it, "I'm Sam Jeckle and been sheriffing for lots of years. The man on my right is the real gunner amongst us, Austin Purdy, straight-shooter, fast-shooter, don't-miss shooter who belongs on your side all the time and never on the other side of the smallest argument."

Purdy touched his Stetson, partly in salute.

Jeckle paused as the words seemed to gain some momentum, a sense of credibility, announcing confidence itself, for the town's rustling disturbances had gotten louder, more evident. A door closed shut at a distance, a horse kicked at a wooden stall from the darkness.

Silence came for moments, as visitors and townsmen continued examinations, the dimmest of inspections.

The man identified as Sam Jeckle, a name known by locals and the general territory, continued his introductions, adding, "The man on my left is Sagamore Joe Ventry, swearing he carries the real American blood in his veins and is damned proud of it, and he's the quietest of the three of us until the fun starts. He can do one thing more ways than a squad of soldiers, and quicker too, and you all know what that is. You *DO* want him on your side is the most testimony I can offer on his part. You sure do."

Those were pretty decent introductions to a small Texas town that was most likely in the gunsights of a band of desperadoes who happened have to hit the town once before, quite successfully, and had come back for a second hit. "Easy pickens of the pie," as might be said.

"Alright, boys," said the official voice, "ride on to the saloon, only a couple of doors down on your left. Eggs are on already." The voice sounded really official even though still unseen.

Still straight up in his saddle, Jeckle said, "What kind of move did they make last time? Their first move, these jackals?"

The official voice replied, "They sent a lone rider into town guaranteeing that more than a dozen citizens would be killed, men, women and kids for sure, if it wasn't a peaceful take-over with help hours away and the roads checked so no one gets out of town."

"He didn't come in the dark, did he?" Jeckle half answered his question.

"No, but he came in the good first light of the morning, so some of us saw him coming in slow, his two pistols in hand, reins loose, like he already owned the place."

"Okay, we're with you," Jeckle said, "but we run the show. Is that a deal?"

The voice in the still darkness said, "Fine by me, fine by us. We don't want to lose anybody, no more bodies in the street." The voice had finally come across as tired, saying, "You run the show. We agree." Those words were almost followed by a *"Whooh"* or a similar expression of relief.

The brigand rider and emissary did indeed come at first good light, riding slowly into town, brandishing two pistols catching first light, slow and comfortable in his approach.

Sam Jeckle walked at him from the side of a building, a shotgun pointing directly at the rider's chest, and Jeckle's most serious voice saying, "Drop both weapons or you're dead where you sit, dead before you hit the ground."

"The boss isn't going to like this," came a lone retort.

"He won't find that out from you 'cause you'll be dead and it's comin' at you quicker than hell lest them two pistols ain't on the ground before I count to One." He had raised one finger into the air.

The two pistols fell upon road dust.

Jeckle said to one of his companions, "Sagamore, strip him down to his drawers, tell the ladies not to look at him, and send him back to where he come from, and best be quick 'cause we don't want any ladies goin' all to blushin'."

The stripped messenger, without proper attire and without his weapons, galloped out of town.

Jeckle said, "Austin, you go off to the right, Sagamore, you go to the left, and I'll hit up the middle. Raise all the hell you can as soon as you can. I don't think they'll be on guard for any surprises. I want the big man, their honcho, hurtin' but healthy when we bring him back here to the folks of this town once did over by them scoundrels from Hell itself."

It was his turn to touch his Stetson, then he advised the now-exposed official voice, a sheriff of some order, "You gents stand pat and wait for us. We'll be back, hopefully with good luck riding with us."

It was perhaps twenty minutes later when single shots, an array of them, seemed to come from different places outside of town. Then rifle sounds came, and several flurries of gunfire from two distinct points of the wide range and slow hills of the area, sounding like a small war, or a singular battle.

One town resident, sitting his horse like he was ready to light out of town, said to the sheriff, "If those new friends of ours have bit the dust, we sure as hell are goin' to pay for it. There's no two ways about that. Them other bozos from last time will string this town up by its neck and let us all dangle off the ground."

For the better part of another twenty minutes, more scattered shots, both rifle and pistol shots, echoed back across the wide grass and the small run of hills that ran around Broken Hill itself.

Mothers chased children back into small homes. "You get in there and stay there like I said or I'll slap your bottom silly." The choices were not many for refusals, denials, but whip, slap, or bottom beatings. All for the unknown ahead of them; in the midst of all this, it was easy to say, there was no place else to go.

Patience, worry, despair, abject terror in some quarters of Broken Hill, managed to be known, expressed, even counted by some town folks in extremes. And the sheriff was unable to alleviate any of it, with simple words. He realized some physical proof had to be seen by folks of the town that they were not going to be harassed to near death by a take-over from the wild bunch out there fighting off a mere three men when his own town cold not mount any threat at all against those terrorists.

He too waited for physical results, some show of success on the part of three strangers who had approached a worried town with a notice of service, of salvation itself, no matter the cost of their own participation.

He heard the opposites sides of results, as if a referee or other official was announcing the results: "Broken Hill zero, bandits all," or "Broken Hill plus, bandits nil." Otherwise, it could be much more serious. Death and devastation loomed as images, as reality, and his mind let him down.

He would not dare to dream further, caught up in his own doubts, caught up in results; they pinned him to a final stillness.

Jeckle, it was, who road back into town from the final silence out and beyond, a big man, almost too big for the saddle he sat, riding beside him, bound in ropes and bandages of a crude sort set on wounds, an official pair of handcuffs in place on his wrists in spite of the gathering of tight ropes binding the balance of him.

115

There was no escaping for this man.

"You know him, Sheriff?" said Jeckle, a half-smile on his face, like an answer before the question.

"That's Howie Kruick's son, Otto, who used to get the Hell beat out of him by his father and we ended up having to pay for it."

"Where's Howie Kruick now?" Jeckle was leaning in his saddle, waiting the answer.

"With the Devil himself," said the son.

Harriet Linwood, big, bony but a solid worker from the first ounce of her sweat, was a born worrier, told her husband Arnold, "I don't trust John Tealer a second longer than a breath. He's been too involved in his land deals, like deals not ever recorded in the territorial offices, and people finding out that they've never owned the land they believed they had purchased from him, sometimes for unbelievable long stretches, and worked it often until death parted them. I've heard some awful stories that have happened to folks like us. Mark my words, if you make this deal, he'll find a way to kill it one way or another."

She hung her rake on a hook on the barn wall, as if the day was done.

Normally she would have turned her back and gotten back to her business of the hour whatever it was, but Arnold Linwood was smiling at her warning, and replied, "I'm not the current dumbbell on his land, Harriet. I've kept my eyes and ears open every damned second we've worked the land on a friendly deal until he proposed this sale to us. If you really want to know what I know, pay attention to what I tell you now."

With that said, and the matter of his mind now also in her possession, she was prepared to support his decision to buy the land they had rented for several years at minimal cost. They earned enough income to build an account at the bank in Tealersburg, where just about every lock, stock and barrel was in Tealer's name ... or getting damned closer to it with each deposit made, note signed and witnessed and sent on its way ... some, as it has been said, accidentally, erroneously or more purposely diverted from its honest intent.

She had always believed that cheating was as bad as outright theft; no difference in the manner of the deed.

Tealer, the tales say, and often from first-hand listeners, would commission a hired gun-hand to "make sure that the delivery boy bound for the Territorial Offices either never gets to that site or coughs up his written dispatch into your hand and thus into my hand, else no currency comes your way; that's when you go payless, son, and owing me, which you do not want to do. Not ever." The venom in his voice was more snake-like than a cobra wiggling its way between bars of a cage.

When Tealer came to propose the deal, he said I'll even let your wife write out the sale deal on paper just the way you want it said. It can't be any better than that, in your own word so it can be declared at the Territorial Offices. Nice and neat and it can't be beat." His humor and fun were constant, just as if he was playing a game.

"It could be that easy," Arnold Linwood said, "but I'm 12 dollars short for the deal. It might take me a bit to sell something to make up the difference."

"You got horses hereabouts, ain't you? I'd buy a horse for 12 dollars." He leaned over and said, 'Any one of them and it would make the deal. Have your wife make up that sale deal also and I'll give you the 12 dollars right now. That a deal too?" His smile was as wide as it could get.

His hand was in his pocket and came out with a fold of bills that could choke all three of them.

"Suits me," offered up Arnold. "You heard the man, Harriet. Draw up that paper too. Do it first so we can do the second one right after the first deal."

Twelve dollars came across the table. Arnold said, "I'll add this to my account and the deal can be swung."

"Good lord, Arnold," Harriet said, "you'll have me doing all the secretarial work for the whole territory. Why, I'd be going from dawn to dusk at that rate."

Tealer, joining in the glee, said, "You could do it like picking up sticks, Ma'am." The laughter was shared around the table. "Make out that land deal paper saying it like you want it said, and I'll sign it right now. No sense in wasting time. Save me another trip out here. But you, sir, have to make the deposit at the bank and get that deal paper up to the Territorial Office. That'll take up a hunk of your time, that being two days on the trail."

"Oh. I won't make that run. I'll get one of the local cowboys to do that on his next ride up the trail."

"Any one of them in particular?"

"Naw," replied Arnold Linwood. "I trust every one of them to deliver an important piece of paper. But, hell," he added as a qualifier, "half or more of them can't read a cook book if they was starving."

The laughter and joy among such confidants was contagious.

They parted company after all documents were signed and witnessed and Tealer left with an old horse that wouldn't make its next run all the way.

But a deal was a deal.

A few days later, after he had deposited the last twelve dollars into his account at the bank, sure that he was being eyed at every move in town by one or more pair of eyes, Arnold Linwood dropped into the saloon to say hello to a few friends and the friendly barkeep, Georgie Willard.

"How you doing today, Georgie? Keeping all accounts square? Harriet said to say hello to you especially for her, but I've been working her somewhat hard these last few days." He made sure his words were heard, and then leaned over and whispered, "Which one of them out here in this bunch would you trust the most on a mission, Georgie. I mean, really trust. It's important to Harriet and me."

"Easy for me to say, Arnie. Greg Wilson is the truest in the bunch. Trust my life in his hands. He's one of the real stand-up gents."

"You get Wilson's ear, Georgie, and let him know I need a good man for an errand and tell him, any chance he gets, to get close to me at this bar. I'll be down at the far end."

It didn't take more than an hour for Greg Wilson to pat Arnold Linwood on the back and offer a loud hello and a welcome back to the bar as if they had been friendly for years.

Georgie brought them a couple of drinks and said, "On the house for old friends," he whispered, and added, "He's special, Greg, just like you are, so pay attention and do the good deed, whatever it is, knowing that it counts for him and his wife Harriet toiling on the land it seems forever." The use of her name seemed to add significance to the errand about to be outlined.

Arnold explained the task at hand, then said, "I'm going to give you a piece of paper, an important one, the one to be delivered to the Territorial Land Office, so slip it into your shirt pocket without even showing the move in the mirror."

The transaction was made securely, secretly, and Arnold then said, "The next one I give to you, make an open move of sticking it in your back pocket so every gent in this place can see where it goes. Nice and open, like it's nothing at all."

And so, it was set up for the long run, from one hand to another to another and yet to be given to another, all in the matter of a few days, to be countable, registered, legal and numbered as such for posterity, future, death and finality, all of which would eventually take place according to higher wills and lower acceptances.

When Greg Wilson, on his next drive up country a few days later, was halfway to the destination of the herd on the move, he was alone in a most inappropriate hollow out of sight of other herders, when a strange gunman, with a quick drop on him, said, "Give me that paper in your back pocket."

The pistol in his hand was waved in Wilson's face.

As commanded at gun point, Greg Wilson took the paper out of his back pocket and handed it to the gunman. The gunman handed it back, saying in his sternest voice, "Tell me what it says." An apathetic look crossed his face, as though it was an apology.

Wilson, not reading what it said, but what he had memorized, said, as if reading directly from the paper, "It's an officially-signed and witnessed land deal for a piece of property outside the town where we started from, Tealersburg. There are some signatures here too that are difficult for me to read," but what it really said, in a strong and firm hand, was, "Dear Alice, This note is to inform you that we have purchased the rights to our land and hereby invite you back for the celebration by transmission of a note to follow, from your dearest friends, The Linwoods, newest landowners near Tealersburg."

The gunman stuck the note in his back pocket and slapped Greg Wilson's horse on the rump so that it galloped off over hill and dale. He had already slapped his own rump where the paper was securely placed for the long ride back down the trail.

He was beside the last tree bearing green, in the sparse land between shifting sands of the great desert, when he saw the vultures descending from their high flight. Brigard Chancelor, "Brig" to friends back in the mountains where breathing proved much easier than here in the midst of little life, sat bareback on an Indian pony he had freed from a natural corral behind a blow-down. Chancelor had learned that the horse would obey tugs on his mane and in this manner, he had escaped from sure capture by heading into the desert, with his pistols loaded and a lariat and a canteen he had grabbed on the run.

Brig was not positive who was after him, either renegade Indians or renegade whites out for the kill, looking for guns, clothes, saddles, anything free. He was hoping they'd measure the little he might have against the rigors of a chase in the desert. Perhaps, he also hoped, they were smarter than he thought they were.

The canteen was almost empty and water had to be found. His throat gave significant warnings of impending perils not to be ignored any more than general custom.

Now, arrowed out of the high sky, he saw the vultures drop down ahead of him and out of sight. There was no hesitation on his part; he'd have to check the attraction. It might only be a natural desert kill, but it could be a man caught in the last tremors of life and death, a man like him, on the run from one thing or another. It was easy to see that life was full of such chases; he was proof of it.

He dipped into a slight swale, crested a small hill as much dune as he had imagined, and saw the horde of black birds at the carcass of a horse, the saddle in place. Chancelor, watching them feast on the horse's flesh, stayed in place, now and then looking back over his shoulder for signs of any pursuit.

In less than half an hour the vultures had almost stripped the bones of flesh. Hoping they had done little damage to the saddle, he galloped in on the hungry critters and drove them off. Shortly they were aligned again high overhead on the lift of a thermal, like people waiting to get into church or for a general store to open its doors.

To his everlasting thanks, the saddle was undamaged and did not take him long to get it off the carcass remnants and onto the pony. The pony, not surprising Chancelor, did not like the smell of death that came upon him, but he held the pony in place by hobbling his front legs.

The saddle looked to be a good old Texas saddle, with a high back, one that would have lasted the rider for life, wherever he was. Or if he was. The initials LGT were burned into the pommel textured into the skirts, and the whole rig showed a few years of use. He'd have to look for the owner, see if he had fallen off, had been wounded, died of thirst. He could not tell how the horse had died. He assumed that if the rider was dead out there somewhere the vultures would have gone after him also.

Chancelor only agreed that he would search ahead of him on the trail for the owner, not behind him, not wanting to run into those chasing him, or had been chasing him. The desert, he wished again, might hold them back.

When he rode off, sitting comfortable at last on the pony, the vultures returned to their feeding, and no signs of pursuit appeared on the wide horizon. Chancelor figured his pursuers had backed off because of the desert threats. Ahead of him, near the Barracks Rim, sat a waterhole the old Kiowa, Bent Wing, had told him about earlier in time, the night they had sat outside Knock's Tavern at the junction of three trails in the mountains. Knock himself had introduced Chancelor to Bent Wing, saying, "Listen to all he says, son. He knows more than any ten mountain men I know. He knows mountain and desert, grass and foothills, forest and canyon, like no one else does. And it's all free for you. I saved his life one time and he ain't never forgot it. No sir, not Bent Wing, Kiowa of all Kiowas. You mark every word he says. And he says things that will matter to you sometime down the trail, where things happen to a man the way they have for a thousand years out here, and he knows it all. Count on it. Came down to him from all the shamans that come before him, loading him up."

Knock had shaken his finger right in Chancelor's nose at the end of that discussion. "Don't think him an old Indian blowing steam, boy. Just realize what he says will save your life someday. He ain't talking for nothing, he's talking good 'cause he's still trying to pay me back, being good to friends of mine."

Through Chancelor's mind went the location of half a dozen waterholes in the range of the desert. The markers came back to him from his lessons at the tent of the Kiowa that one night outside Knock's Tavern. "One water hole is like a breath of air in the desert and sits near the Barracks Rim where the old fort used to be. The elder of all shamans told me it runs a thousand feet underground to cleanse itself for thirsty men. Comes clear through the mountain from a high lake the great god made."

Bent Wing told him about more water holes the Kiowa gods had sent to his tribe. "We share what has been given to us. You must do the same."

"Have any of them gone dry?"

"Oh, many. Those that were hidden from a decent thirst were fired dry by an angry god. No man owns a water hole."

Landmarks had been explained to him by Bent Wing, places to look for, to look from, measures to be made, marks that were left for Indian eyes now coming to his eyes. The eagle talon on the face of a rock as he closed on Barracks Rim told him the waterhole was close enough to grasp. He found the slit of water at the base of Barracks Rim, in a cluster of rocks. In half an hour he had filled his canteen. The water had appeared in a slit of rock and disappeared in the rock cluster not pooling up at all. He had never seen one like it and was thankful the old Kiowa had shared its location with him.

As Chancelor prepared to leave he caught sight of a flash of sunlight reflected from a surface down the trail ahead of him. It flashed again and then it flashed again. A minute later it flashed again.

Someone was signaling him. Chancelor looked down at the initials on the saddle, thinking he had found the saddle owner, that he had found LGT.

Chancelor urged the pony toward the flashing source, perhaps a mile away. Behind him there appeared to be no pursuit, and under him the saddle, LGT's saddle, was new to him but comfortable in a few strides of the Indian pony. With nothing behind him, Chancelor wondered what was in front of him. Would he find LGT up there with the reflections, obvious signals for help? If it was the owner of the saddle, he'd be riding bareback again. Perhaps soon.

Perhaps not. The place of the signals he had marked by an overhanging outcrop, a bulge that Bent Wing would have attributed to the Great God pushing on the earth, making new places, new gardens, new forests, and, of course, to test man, new deserts.

From a hundred feet away, he saw the man's arm swing slowly, the way a tired man swings his arm or a wounded man. Chancelor, approaching with caution, knew from about ten feet that the man was wounded. Blood was all over his shirt, one arm solely red. It was not the arm he had waved.

"I'm glad to see you, mister. I thought I'd never get another drink of water. I'm bone dry, near dead, but want a drink of water." Then, after looking at the pony, he said, "I see you found my saddle."

"You LGT?"

With his finger pointing at Chancelor's canteen, he said, "Yes, Logan Thompson. I'm from the Barrel Ranch, the Bar-Circle-B. Got jumped by some renegades and galloped down this way hoping they wouldn't chase me. But a round caught me square from a long way off and I crawled in here as my horse ran off. Must have been hit too."

"What's the G for?"

"Glendor. My father brought it from Australia a long time ago. It's a native name, like he wanted to hold onto something. He jumped ship on the west coast. Was a sailor and became a herder. Had enough of the sea."

Chancelor held the canteen as Thompson took a small sip, then a gulp. "Sorry for taking your water, but it's a swap … you got my saddle." He tried to laugh, but it didn't come out right. He coughed deeply.

"My pals will be looking for me," he said. "If they find you with my saddle you better be able to explain in a hurry why you have it. I can't be any clearer than that. They'll look for me until they find me, no matter what shape I'm in."

He coughed again, and this time it was deep and sounded as if it was not going to let go of him.

He waited until he caught his breath, and Chancelor knew he was in the presence of a tough, tough man, who said, "If I had a pencil and paper I'd write you a bill of sale, my saddle for the best drink of water I ever had, but I haven't got them. If they catch up to you tell them my middle name. That'll be proof enough that I gave it to you. I won't make it out of here, I know that. Tell them my last thoughts find them doing what they like best. You have to swear to that."

"I swear," Chancelor said. "I swear." He raised his hand.

Thompson began a small litany. "One's a singer and writes his own songs, plays great guitar. One would rather fish than anything in the world and then eat the catch at an open fire. He's a dreamer, but a worker like the others. One's a lover, enough said. But they're all good men on a drive. We've been together for a long time. Since we were half a knee high. Be careful, though; they can be impulsive when one of us has been hurt or misjudged or even called a bad name out of turn, the likes of which have started a minor brawl or two in a few saloons."

Besides the coughing, Chancelor knew other things were working down in Thompson. His face grimaced several times, the way one might measure the onslaught of different pains, how deep they went, how long they lasted.

"What are their names?" Chancelor said.

Thompson, about to speak, held one hand up in a pause, took a noisy, deep breath, shook, looked at Chancelor right in the eyes, and died on the spot. Blood ran from his mouth in one gush, and stopped, as if the whole mechanism of the body quit on the spot after a final shiver and shake that ran down his frame.

Always looking around him for signs of danger, checking out every swirl of dust, Chancelor assembled enough rocks and stones and limestone slabs at the foot of the rim to inter LG Thompson from the ravages of animals and vultures. The only mark he left was scratched into the face of the cliff … LGT. A good eye would be able to see the letters.

Thompson's hat, a good Stetson, became Chancelor's, but he left Thompson's boots in place, burying them with the man under the pile of rocks. He did not want to step into the other man's boots, plain and simple.

The Good Words were spoken over the site and Chancelor, with renewed spirit, set off again.

Late in the day, after drifting across an arid stretch of land, he found a break in the cliff face and started the climb to the top of Barracks Rim. At the top, after an arduous trip even for the Indian pony, he was in an instant surrounded by five riders.

"We heard you coming up, mister, so we just waited." The speaker not only sounded mean, he looked mean, as he said, "Tell me where you got that saddle, mister. And you better be clean and quick about it." His hands bore two Smith & Wesson shooters, aimed right at Chancelor. "Say it all slow, mister, but say it all."

"The saddle was given to me by a man named Logan Thompson. I found him wounded down below the rim. He said he was chased by some renegades though he wasn't sure if they were Indians or what. I think it might have been the same ones who chased me, got my horse."

"Where'd you get the pony?"

"He was trapped in the corner of a canyon by a blow-down that cut his escape route. I had to break his way out of there. Those who were chasing me went right past the blow-down and the pony kept quiet. But they might still be after me."

"So, where's this Thompson fella you're talking about?"

"I buried him down below the rim. Marked the wall with his initials, like on his saddle. See, LGT there." He pointed down at the skirt of the saddle.

"Maybe you killed him. How does that sound? How do we know you ain't lying about it all? Even making up the story about him giving you his saddle. Where's his horse?"

"Gone to vulture food," Chancelor replied. "I saw it straight off. They dropped in on the horse like they were shot at it. Half the animal gone when I came close on them."

"Where was the rider?"

"I got the saddle off and put it on the pony and a bit later I saw some flashing from the base of the rim. That's where I found Thompson, been shot bad. Said he'd write me a bill of sale for the saddle but had no pencil."

The reply was still mean. "You could have made it all this up."

"Told me his pards would come. Told me about them. The singer. The lover. The fisherman. That you boys?"

"You could have heard that from anybody who knows us. None of it is secret. We don't know if we'll believe you or not. You got his hat." He looked down at Chancelor's boots after he checked the Stetson. "Where's his boots?"

"On him when I buried him. I didn't need them, but I didn't have a hat."

"Anything else?"

"Told me what 'G' stands for."

"Oh, yah, what for?"

"Said his daddy brought it all the way from Australia when he jumped ship on the coast. Stands for Glendor, some native name."

"That's okay with us then. You sound like you treated Logan square. Let's see where you buried him. We have to say our words for him. He was a good cowpoke, a good friend to all of us. We'll miss him. We'll miss him a lot."

He shifted in the saddle, looked at his pals and said, "Let's take care of this and then tomorrow we'll chase down those coyotes. We'll need a horse for this fella. What's your name, mister?"

"Brigard Chancelor. No middle initial. They call me Brig. I was on my way to a new job in Parkersville."

"For now, Brig, you got another new job."

They all started back down the trail, through the break in the rim, with Chancelor in the lead. They were just about at the bottom when he threw up his hand after he had spotted movement back along the base of the cliff. It was not more vultures but half a dozen riders just about where he had covered Thompson with rocks.

One by one the new friendship team slipped into a low break in the land and moved half way to the group of men working at the burial site.

They were disinterring LG Thompson.

Without a signal of any kind, like a single mind was working, the men charged at the men at the site. The battle did not last long. And one man lived long enough to tell them who he and his pards worked for, and why.

Chancelor, as it turned out, was no longer just along for the ride. He had become one of them and sat the saddle that had always had been part of them.

To a man, Chancelor knew, they would see justice was done, to one and all.

About the Author

Thomas F. Sheehan served in the 31st Infantry, Korea, 1951-52, and graduated Boston College, 1956. Books include *Epic Cures; Brief Cases, Short Spans; The Saugus Book; This Rare Earth & Other Flights; Ah, Devon Unbowed; Reflections from Vinegar Hill*. eBooks include *Korean Echoes (nominated for a Distinguished Military Award)*, *The Westering*, (nominated for National Book Award); from *Danse Macabre* are *Murder at the Forum, Death of a Lottery Foe, Death by Punishment, An Accountable Death and Vigilantes East. A Collection of Friends, From the Quickening, In the Garden of Long Shadows*, *The Nations, Where Skies Grow Wide, Cross Trails, The Cowboys, Between Mountain and River,* and *Beside the Broken Trail* were published by Pocol Press, and *Six Guns, Inc.,* by *Nazar Look,* in Romania. Sheehan has multiple works at these sites: *Rosebud, Linnet's Wings, Serving House Journal, Copperfield Review, KYSO Flash, La Joie Magazine, Soundings East, Literary Orphans, Indiana Voices Journal, Frontier Tales, Western Online Magazine, Provo Canyon Review, Nazar Look, Eastlit, Rope & Wire Magazine, Ocean Magazine, The Literary Yard, Green Silk Journal, Fiction on the Web, The Path, Faith-Hope and Fiction, The Cenacle, etc.* Sheehan's tales have produced 30 Pushcart nominations, and five Best of the Net nominations (and one winner) and short story awards from *Nazar Look* for 2012-2015. *Swan River Daisy* was recently released by KY Stories and *Back Home in Saugus*, 200 pages, 90,000 words, and a chapbook, *Small Victories for the Soul*, are on proposal. (His Amazon Author's Page, Tom Sheehan – is on the Amazon site.)